LAST CRUISE
TO PARADISE

William J. Millman

SB

Sunset Beach Press

SB

Sunset Beach Press

Manufactured in the United States of America

Cover photos: inmagine.com, ginosphotos

ISBN: 978-0692440667

To Rob: Brady James' First Fan

(with a nod to Ms. Christie)

CHAPTER 1

The cool afternoon breeze carried a hint of rain to the upper deck of the Fantasy Princess as it approached its first stop of a seven-day cruise: the island paradise of Bermuda. The 110,000 ton ocean liner had departed Baltimore the evening before, carrying among its nearly 3500 passengers the usual assortment of honeymooners, once-in-a-lifetime vacationers, cruise addicts and, oh yes, one diminutive private investigator by the name of Derek DiLaurain.

"Oh Derek," a six-foot blonde by the name of Olga sighed contentedly as she stared out across the dark expanse of Atlantic Ocean in the general direction of the island paradise, "this even better than I hope." Olga's English was less than outstanding, but her statuesque form and piercing blue eyes left nothing to be desired. At least not for Derek.

"Stick with me, baby," he said, utilizing his best Bogart impression. "You'll go places." He patted her tight, rounded backside without even realizing that he had to reach up to do so. He was a little person, always had been. But that didn't keep him from appreciating the bigger things in life, starting with tall women. Olga bent down and planted a kiss on the PI's forehead, leaving an imprint of bright red lips as well-defined as if they'd been tattooed on his tanned skin by some crazed ink doctor.

Derek had only known Olga for a few weeks, having identified her as 'the other woman' in a particularly nasty divorce case he'd worked on. 'Particularly nasty divorce' – an oxymoron where he was concerned. If the relationship had disintegrated to the extent that one of the two aggrieved parties had called him in to dig dirt, it was almost always nasty. The money was good, but Derek didn't particularly enjoy that part of his practice. In fact, Olga had been the only bright spot in a dreary month of tails, long-range photos, and quasi-legal buggings. At first she'd been furious with him for upsetting her gravy-train, at one point screaming what he could only assume were vile Russian obscenities at him in the middle of a high-class hotel lobby in DC. He later learned she'd been afraid that she'd be deported if the authorities learned she was in the States illegally. But as time went on, and no jackbooted authorities came knocking on her door, she came to understand that even a little guy sometimes had hidden gifts that could make it well worth her while to reconsider her hasty evaluation, and they'd grown closer quickly. Very close, very quickly.

As he stared up at her with the first twinkling stars beginning to appear in the deep blue canopy above her head, his thoughts wandered to a shrink he'd once worked for who'd told him he was 'compensating' by always dating tall women. He'd told the old quack that 1) he should mind his own business; and 2) if Derek was going to put up with the infinite idiosyncrasies of the female of the species, he might as well get his money's worth. His business relationship with the doctor in question had ended rather precipitously.

The cruise was something of a test drive, a solid week trapped onboard one of the more luxurious ships to ply that particular itinerary with the lovely Olga. Perhaps 'trapped' is too strong a term. At least for the first day the proximity had been mutually satisfying. As far as he could tell. Reading a woman was like trying to read a scientific manual in a foreign language. Make that an obscure, complex, nearly incomprehensible foreign language.

From just about ear level Derek thought he heard a loud grumbling sound.

"Getting hungry?"

"Da."

Though not the natural polyglot, the PI had picked up enough Russian to get by. Barely. Olga still launched into the occasional monologue that left him utterly bewildered, usually when he'd pissed her off. But for the most part, she slaughtered English and he massacred Russian, and they got along just fine.

"What do you say we head down to the dining room then and grab a bite?"

"Grab bite?" Her scrinched-up eyes and pouting lips when he used a slang term she didn't understand never ceased to tickle him.

"Eat dinner," he explained with an understanding smile.

"Khorosho."

That meant 'okay,' or at least he thought it did. He tugged her by the hand until she bent down to where he could plant a kiss on those brilliant red lips.

"*Very* khorosho," he said, and with a wink led her to a stairway that took them down to the dining area.

Early diners already jammed the vast room, comprised – for the most part – of families with kids and older folks who wanted to make sure they finished their desserts before they nodded off. Derek didn't really care how crowded the main room got because he'd already staked out a small private alcove in the back and secured it with a $20 tip to the maître d' on their first night aboard. So when the very same harried maître d' met them at the entrance to the room, they expected to be seated immediately. They were mistaken.

"Sorry, Mr. DiLaurain," the maître d' said with tightly-pursed lips. "We've got a special function." He nodded his head toward the back of the room, where Derek could see a sizeable area blocked off by stanchions and velvet ropes. A large gathering was seated around a long, elegantly set table, with a smaller table off to one side populated by small children overseen by a couple of adult chaperones. At the far end of the long table a very old man sat propped-up in a wheelchair, withered to little more than skin and bones, his old-fashioned black glasses seemingly oversized for the shrunken face beneath them.

"What's up?" the PI asked, trying with only modest success to keep his displeasure hidden.

"It's Mr. Geist and his family," the man whispered, looking around as if afraid to be overheard. "It's his birthday."

Olga saw Derek's eyes narrow and grabbed his shoulder reflexively. From previous interactions, she knew that Derek had a tendency to take slights personally. She thought it might have something to do with his stature.

"They find us good table," she said softly, and then turning to the maître d' added, "right?"

"Of course, of course! If you can just give me a few moments…"

"Let me understand you," the PI interjected, his voice suffering no interruption. "I gave you $20 to hold a table for my lady friend and me, and now – the very next night – you tell me it's not available?! Who the hell *is* this Geist guy?"

The cruise employee waved his hands to cool down the irate customer. "Please! He is a *very* wealthy man. Real estate, I believe."

"*Arnold* Geist?" DiLaurain asked, standing on tip-toe to try to better see the celebration at the back of the dining room.

"The very same. *And* his entire family. They are celebrating his 90th birthday."

"Hmmph," Derek grumbled. "This better be just one night."

"Just tonight, I assure you," the maître d' sputtered, overjoyed at seeing a way out of the conundrum he faced. "For the rest of our cruise, your table will be sacrosanct."

"We don't want to pray, just eat in peace," Derek said with a grimace, and Olga relaxed her death grip on his shoulder. "All right. I guess what's done is done. Do we get a table, or do we have to stand here all night?"

The maître d' jumped as if hit by lightning. "Of course, of course you shall have a table!" he cried, his eyes suddenly alert. "Samuel!" he called out, waving to a small, dark-skinned waiter in a white server's jacket.

"Please show Mr. DiLaurain and his lovely friend to D-34." Derek could've sworn he detected a hint of a French accent, something that hadn't surfaced in any of their earlier meetings. The man's relieved smile drew a sneer from Derek and an equally insincere nod from Olga.

"Money talks," Derek said to her as they picked their way through the crowded room.

"In Russia, we have saying," Olga replied. "Всего с собой не унесёшь."

"What the hell does that mean?"

Olga had a tendency to lapse into Russian whenever she wanted to make a point.

"Even rich man can't take money when die," she translated.

"I think that's one of ours."

"Российский."

"Whatever."

The waiter led them to a small, two-person table all the way in the back of the room, not far from the double swinging doors that led to the kitchen.

"Didn't you have anything in a lifeboat, or maybe the engine room?" Derek jibed.

"We are *very* crowded just now. If you had come a bit earlier, or even later…" the waiter explained apologetically.

"How about November? Is it crowded in November?"

The waiter looked at him dumbstruck, not quite sure how to answer.

"Never mind," Derek waved him off. "Here – get us some wine that doesn't taste like the goat piss they serve to the rest of these poor schmucks," he directed, passing the man a twenty.

"Red, or white?"

"Just make it good."

The waiter was instantly all smiles and light. "Of course, monsieur," he answered, his French coming across as a blend of Spanish and Filipino. He bowed ever so slightly and trotted off at once.

"Not his fault," Olga said as the waiter disappeared from sight.

"I gave him a twenty!" Derek countered. "What did you want – a hundred buck tip for just doing his job?"

The conversation devolved from there, until the effects of a bottle of Cotes du Rhone Parallele 45 put the two vacationers in a more appropriate mood. Even Derek had to admit the food was halfway decent, and more than plentiful. Olga barely ate a thing, however, preferring to stick to the calories in the excellent red instead of the mountainous buffet.

"Sure I can't get you anything?" Derek asked as he headed back to the buffet line for thirds.

"Nyet, Спасибо."

"You know I paid for this food, whether you eat it or not."

"Tomorrow maybe."

He shrugged. He wasn't about to argue with an eating regimen that produced a figure like Olga's. If she wanted to eat nothing but breadsticks and wine, it was okay with him. As he made his way to the bustling buffet area, he glanced none-too-subtly back at the Geist birthday party, trying to get a sense of how the filthy rich celebrated such a milestone event. Of course, it was difficult to get a good view from his low-angle perspective, but he did his best to catch a glimpse through passing crotches and the occasional break between tables.

At one point he stood transfixed as a good old-fashioned verbal brawl seemed to break out, with a few of the middle-aged participants seeming to gang up on the old man and his wife.

'Good to see even the rich have family problems,' he thought as he continued on to the buffet.

One of the things he liked about this cruise line was that their buffet tables were lower than others he'd sailed with, just about at (his) eye level. With the least bit of a stretch, on tip-toe, he could reach nearly everything he wanted. Anything else, he feigned disinterest or – if it was something he simply couldn't do without – he asked a waiter to help him drag it to his plate.

He was in the midst of doing just that – dragging a piece of rare roast beef from a pseudo-silver serving tray, when two relatively loud, unmistakably angry voices came down to him from the heavens above.

"That old bastard just loves screwing us around," one male voice announced.

"Always has," the other agreed.

"One of these days…" the first went on.

"He'll get what's coming to him. If he doesn't kick the bucket first."

Eavesdropping is an occupational predilection with private investigators, and so it was understandable that Derek tried to linger at his place in line as long as possible to hear what had motivated the exchange. Unfortunately, he lingered a bit too long and one of the two complainers stepped on his foot.

"Hey, take it easy!" he cried out, his left instep burning from the giant boat that had tried to dock on his relatively tiny port.

"What the hell?!" the man answered, his words slurred from one too many dinner drinks. "Oh. Didn' see you down there." He looked past the plate he held in one hand, his expression of bemused surprise all too familiar to Derek. His deep-set brown eyes twinkled in a jowly, sunburned face that might once have been considered modestly handsome. Now the wrinkles and blotches made it look like a map that someone had spilled coffee on and then crumpled up in disgust.

"How's the weather down there?" the other guy joined-in, his smile even broader and less sympathetic. He was taller than his buddy and 30 or 40 pounds lighter, with the same brown eyes and broad, pulpy nose. Brilliant white hair made him look older than Derek thought him to be, which was somewhere around 60. On second glance, Derek decided they might be related.

"It *was* fine," he answered with barely feigned good nature.

"I said I was sorry," the first guy whined with the tone of maligned self-importance that the PI despised.

"Yeh, you're a prince," Derek shot back.

"Hey, listen you little piece of..."

The white-haired guy grabbed him by the arm. "Don't listen to him," he said to Derek, "my brother's just pissed-off that our old man's an asshole."

"Must run in the family," the PI growled.

"'Run in the family!' Hey, that's pretty good."

"For a midget," the heavier guy added with a lopsided smirk.

"'For a midget!'" his brother repeated with undeserved enthusiasm. "That's pretty good too."

Just then, Derek remembered why he'd promised himself he'd never take another cruise after his last 10-day jaunt: you were stranded on a floating Vegas motel with dozens of screaming kids, bedazzled hicks, and a small army of drunken assholes like these two. He managed to bite-back a purposefully pungent riposte and waddled away with his roast beef in-hand.

He heard the two brothers chuckling and mumbling behind him, but didn't want to give them the satisfaction of a reaction. Despite his best efforts, he was red-faced and steaming when he got back to his table.

"What?! What is?" Olga asked when she saw his expression.

"The usual," he answered through clenched teeth. "Stupid assholes."

"Screw on them," his girlfriend said, stroking his hair soothingly. "They don't know their ass from hole in wall."

Derek smiled in spite of himself. "You have a way with words," he said.

She arched her eyebrows and leered. "Have other ways too," she whispered conspiratorially. "Will show you when get back to cabin."

"It's a date," he said, digging into his roast beef with a renewed appetite.

It was nearly an hour – and another bottle of the '45' – later, when the two of them finished their meal and swayed their way back to their cabin, each supporting the other.

"Now what was that about other talents'?" he asked as soon as the outer door closed.

"You see. Get in bed. I come in few minutes."

"I hope it takes longer than that!" he called after her as she disappeared into the bathroom. And when it came right down to it, it did.

CHAPTER 2

Derek was in his big pig of a Caddy, cruisin' down I-395, Olga beside him, her hair whipping wildly in the breeze from the open windows. They were both laughing, having a good ol' time.

"Is good — yes?" she asked when she caught her breath.

"Very," he answered. "You're a very talented girl."

"Russian women have many talent."

"So I've noticed."

"You not see half."

"Like what?" he asked, the dare evident in his voice.

She smiled at him, her eyebrows tilting like a sensual Groucho Marx. "Just drive."

She bent down, her long blonde hair nearly becoming entangled in the steering wheel. He heard the grating sound of a zipper and felt his Little Friend begin to grow.

And then...

A knock dragged him back to wakefulness. Soft, but persistent.

"God damn!" he muttered to himself, throwing the covers back and dragging himself out of the nice warm bed. Olga lay beside him, dead to the world. "I'm coming, I'm coming," he whispered, loud enough to stop the knocking but not so loud as to wake his Ruskie amazon. He slipped into a dark blue silk travel robe and took a quick peek in the mirror by the door to straighten his incredibly disheveled hair. He glanced at the clock on a nearby side table: 5:45.

"This better be good," he said as he pulled open the door.

He didn't know what to expect, but an attractive middle-aged woman in a Princess business suit wasn't it.

"Mr. DiLaurain?" the woman asked politely. "I'm so very sorry to bother you at this early hour."

All of Derek's steam leaked out in one long, resigned sigh. "No problem. I was… almost awake anyway. What can I do for you?"

The woman glanced up and down the hallway anxiously.

"My girlfriend's still asleep," Derek said, nodding back toward his cabin as if to explain why he couldn't invite her inside.

"Of course, of course. It's just… well, this is an *extremely* sensitive matter."

The PI racked his mind: had his cruise payment bounced?

"You see," the woman continued, "I'm Caroline Earthal – the ships' security officer?" She looked at him as if he might recognize the name. He didn't. "Yes, well, we have a… situation that I was hoping you might be able to help us with."

"Me? What kind of situation?" If nothing else, she'd piqued his interest.

The woman stopped and stared down at Derek as if weighing her options. "You *are* the Derek DiLaurain who works for Brady James, aren't you?"

"*With*. I work *with* James."

"Oh good, I thought so, but you can never be certain…"

"The situation?" Derek prompted.

"Yes, well…" She looked as if she might cry. "It's Mr. Geist – Arnold Geist – he's… disappeared!"

Derek had been a private investigator for nearly twenty years and had worked untold numbers of cases of people who'd 'disappeared'. Most of them were just somewhere they weren't supposed to be. A few didn't want to be found. Fewer still had come to a bad end. He thought about chastising the foolish woman for waking him up at such an ungodly hour, but decided to play the good guy for a change.

"Have you searched the ship?" he asked, trying not to let sarcasm slip into his voice.

"Top to bottom. We've had half our staff looking all night," she said with the slightest hint of panic.

"Right. And I suppose you asked his family if anyone had seen him."

"No one. Not since the big announcement."

Derek wanted nothing more than to creep back into bed and surprise Olga with a special wake-up call, but professional curiosity and personal nosiness got the better of him. "It sounds like there's a story here. Is there someplace we can go to discuss it?" he asked.

"My office?"

"Good. Let me get some clothes on and I'll meet you there in ten minutes." He turned to go back into his room but stopped mid-stride. "Uh, where exactly is this office?"

She told him it was on B deck, at the far end of the administrative offices.

"Okay then, see you there."

Derek took pains to creep around the cabin as quietly as possible, but still managed to shave and throw on some passable clothes in a matter of minutes. As he slipped out of the cabin he pulled the door gently shut to the sounds of Olga's heavy breathing. He hesitated a second to visualize the not-so-little surprise he had planned to deliver as a wake-up call, but then surrendered to the inevitable and padded off down the hallway. He barely glanced out at the docks where the cruise ship had berthed sometime during the night.

Ms. Earthal's office was one deck above Derek's cabin, on a level that contained a bar, a small showroom, and some of the nicest suites on the ship. Derek barely noticed the finery, however, as he made his way directly to the security suite.

"Oh, thank you so much for coming at this hour," Ms. Earthal gushed as soon as he came through the door. "This could really become a major embarrassment for the cruise line."

"Could be worse than that for old Mr. Geist if he doesn't turn up."

"Of course, of course," the security chief covered her gaffe as best she could. Two other Princess employees, both young, muscular men in dark blue blazers standing on either side of Caroline's desk, tried unsuccessfully to disguise their surprise upon seeing Derek. The tiny PI gave each man a quick nod of acknowledgement before scanning the office. The first of two rooms was a large space filled with modern overstuffed chairs and a sofa, resembling a living room more than a traditional office; only the substantial dark wood desk spoke to the business requirements of the space. Through an open door toward the back of the office he could see a more spare environment, with two small metal desks and a fax machine nestled close together beneath stark florescent lighting.

"Can I get you anything? Coffee?" Earthal asked the PI.

"Yeh, thanks. I could use a jolt of caffeine to get the ol' heart beating."

"Hungry?"

"I think I could eat."

She picked up the phone on her desk and punched a single button. "Jason? Good morning," she said into the receiver. "Could we have a full breakfast set-up for four here in my office? Great, thanks."

As soon as she'd hung up the phone, she turned to the young man on her right. "Todd, why don't you fill Mr. DiLaurain in on the details of Mr. Geist's disappearance."

"Mr. DiLaurain, as I'm sure you're aware, Arnold Geist is a very influential businessman," Todd began with a bit more pomposity and self-importance than Derek preferred.

"He's a rich old SOB, that's for sure," the PI responded to bring the situation into a more appropriate perspective.

The nonplussed young security operative glanced over at his boss. She signaled him to continue. "Yes… well, he was onboard the Princess with his entire family to celebrate his 90th birthday."

"And," the other blue-blazered bookend chimed-in with a conspiratorial tone that made Derek want to slap him, "to learn the details of Mr. Geist's last will and testament."

"Oh?" Derek said with increased interest. Maybe this wasn't going to be such a dull affair after all.

"Let Todd continue, Eric," Ms. Earthal ordered somewhat testily. Eric rolled his eyes but complied.

"That's right," the first assistant confirmed. "They were all here to learn who would inherit what when Mr. Geist passes."

"No wonder there were arguments," Derek remarked, as much to himself as the three Princess employees.

"There were arguments?" Caroline asked, leaning forward with sudden interest.

"No one mentioned the drag-out knock-downs among the family members at dinner last night?"

The security chief glanced at her two underlings, who looked to each other for insight. None was forthcoming.

"No? Did you interview any of the family members?"

"We... spoke to his wife and two of his children," Caroline explained. "But all our efforts were centered on searching the ship." She was clearly covering her backside.

"And none of the three you talked to said a word about the shouting match at the dinner table?" The PI didn't hide his incredulity.

"Not that I remember," Ms. Earthal answered. Tweedle Dumb and Tweedle Dumber shook their heads woodenly.

"Strange. Maybe there's more to this 'disappearance' than I thought."

"What do you mean?!" Caroline asked, coming half out of her seat with nervous energy. "Surely you don't suspect foul play?" The terrified look on her face almost made Derek laugh.

"I *always* suspect foul play," he said. "Especially when you're talking about a billion or so good reasons."

"I'm certain Mr. Geist will show up," Todd said with little enthusiasm.

"They always do," Eric added with a small child's hopefulness.

"You're probably right," Derek agreed. He'd learned long before that it was easier to go along with the powers-that-be. At least until the facts on the ground proved them wrong. "But whatever it turns out to be, if I'm working this case I'd like to talk to Mrs. Geist again – and some of their children."

"Do you really think that's necessary, Mr. DiLaurain?" the security head asked. "I mean, it's already been quite traumatic for them all."

"Do you want to find the old man?" He eyed each one of them individually.

"Well, of course," Caroline answered for all three.

"Then, yes, I think it's necessary. Think any of them are awake at this ungodly hour?"

"Mrs. Geist has already called this morning," Todd chirped. "She wanted to know if we'd learned anything more about her husband's disappearance."

"Then I'll start with her. Could you contact her to see when she might be available for an interview?"

A sharp knock on the cabin door was followed immediately by a waiter pushing a metal cart loaded down with enough food for a half-dozen burly loggers.

"Will you have something to eat before you get started?" Caroline asked.

Derek was about to ask if bears defecate in the woods, but thought better of it. "Love to," he said instead.

Within minutes the expensive glass coffee table that fronted the even more expensive glove leather sofa had been transformed into a serviceable breakfast counter, complete with white linen placemats and matching napkins.

"You always eat like this?" he asked as he drizzled warm maple syrup over a picture-perfect Belgian waffle topped by absolutely flawless strawberries.

"Only when it's business," Todd answered between forkfuls of eggs Benedict. The PI figured there were a lot of *business* meals on their expense accounts.

Over a surprisingly leisurely meal, Derek questioned the three Princess security people about the ship, about what they knew of the Geist family, and anything else that might help them find the patriarch of the family. It turns out that Geist wasn't a stranger to the Princess line – one of the more luxurious of the many large cruise lines that plied the Caribbean, or to the Fantasy itself, for that matter. He and his wife, Ida, were regulars on the cruise circuit, having set sail at least two or three times a year for the past ten years or more. Usually they sailed alone, or in recent years – as the old man's health deteriorated, with just his nurse. Occasionally with a grandchild or two. None of the three could remember the Geist children accompanying their parents.

"How were they regarded by the staff?" Derek asked as he sipped his exotic Colombian Supremo/ Sumatran Mandheling blend coffee.

"We really cannot discuss internal staff opinions," Caroline answered primly.

"Do you want to find the old man, or not?" the PI growled. He understood privacy concerns as well as the next person, but he also understood what impact the disappearance of an important man like Geist would have on the cruise line's bottom line.

Derek watched an entire spectrum of emotions play out across the security chief's face. But before she could come to a decision on whether to speak out or not, Todd made the decision for her.

"He can be a real prick," the young staffer said off-handedly.

"Todd!" his boss chastised, "we do NOT characterize our passengers in that fashion!"

Todd shrugged.

"The wife is okay," Eric added, perhaps to take some of the spotlight off his partner. "Kind of quiet."

"That will be quite enough!" Caroline shouted. Even she seemed surprised by her outburst.

"Mr. Geist is one of our most highly-regarded passengers. If he sometimes has… difficult moments, it's perfectly understandable. I'm sure he's doing the best he can under difficult circumstances."

"Like what?" Derek asked casually. It didn't seem that a retired billionaire could have all that many problems.

"He's been ill for quite some time, now," Caroline answered. "At least five or six years."

"And that family of his…" Todd began, but a sharp look from Caroline stopped him cold.

"Not the most loving and lovable bunch, is that it?"

"Every family has its difficulties," Caroline jumped in before either of her two young associates could expand on the subject. "Some of the younger family members are easier to deal with than others."

"Look, I understand the need for confidentiality," the PI said. "What's discussed here won't go beyond these walls." *Except perhaps to Brady James.* "But if Mr. Geist's disappearance is more than just an old guy getting lost on a big ship, I'll need to know as much as possible about the dynamics of the family if I'm going to be able to help you find out what happened to him. Understand?" The vast majority of cases he investigated ended up involving either a close friend or a family member. In his experience most people were overly terrified about bad guys when they should be more concerned about those closest to them.

Caroline pursed her lips as she weighed her options. "Okay. All right, but all this is *completely* off-the-record, understood?"

Derek nodded. "Understood."

With that the floodgates opened. Turned out that although Mr. Geist may have been one of the line's most highly-regarded passengers, he definitely wasn't one of their favorites.

"The old man orders everyone around as if they're his personal servants," Todd explained. "He never smiles and rarely says thanks."

"We all wonder how his wife puts up with it."

"And his nurse. She must be a saint."

"His kids are the worst. At least the old man's sick. The kids don't have any reason for being such horses' asses."

Caroline blanched but didn't say a word. Her two young assistants more than made up for her reticence.

In a few minutes Derek had a much clearer picture of the Geist family. His initial hunch that the old man's disappearance might be more than just a case of taking a wrong turn seemed increasingly likely. He'd been a PI for a long time. He could smell bad news a mile away. This case stunk to high heavens.

CHAPTER 3

When the briefing finally came to a close, Derek raised the delicate topic of remuneration, and was pleasantly surprised when Ms. Earthal met his demands without blinking. *'Should've asked for more,'* he thought with a shrug. He requested Internet access and was directed to a desk in the back, complete with a fancy laptop connected to a 23 inch monitor. The PI felt like he was at a drive-in movie when the computer sprang to life. He searched a number of sites to find out all he could about Mr. Geist and his family, including a couple of costly proprietary information providers that Brady insisted they subscribe to.

There wasn't too much he didn't already know about Geist: self-made billionaire, real estate tycoon with an enormous ego, conservative political campaign donor. Not much at all about his wife, Ida. Just a few articles about some charity work she'd done for a children's hospital. Appeared to keep a low profile. Derek wondered whether that was her doing or her husband's.

Then there were the kids: Arnold Jr, the oldest, was apparently a chip off the old block, only more so. He'd taken control of the old man's holding company when Arnold Sr. 'retired' at age 75, and had increased its net worth by nearly a billion dollars in under 15 years. He seemed to love the limelight, as the PI found an extensive listing of TV, radio and assorted other media appearances. Junior was married, with three kids of his own. Ayden, the middle Geist son, was something of a cipher. Derek could find only a handful of listings for the man, most of which dealt with a non-profit he'd created to find a cure for some obscure disease that afflicted his daughter. He had one other child, a boy, and seemed to be the antithesis of his father and older brother.

The most interesting of the sons was Aaron. Nearly twenty years younger than his oldest brother, Aaron was something of a wild man, a single playboy with a reputation for fast cars, fast boats, and fast women. Not necessarily in that order. Of particular interest, at least to Derek, he'd recently had some "financial reversals" according to a Monte Carlo newspaper, and his credit was no longer unassailable in the local casinos. Derek printed out the article.

About a half-hour later, Todd came back to tell him that Mrs. Geist was now available and was expecting him – in 15 minutes.

"That doesn't give me much time to change," the PI complained.

"Don't worry – she's not one of the stuffy ones. She won't mind."

"If you say so."

Fifteen minutes later, his hair somewhat less disheveled but the rest of him in the same condition as when he'd eaten breakfast, the PI stood outside the Geist suite of rooms accompanied by Todd. They could hear the doorbell chime inside the cabin, and in seconds a short but very trim and attractive 20-something woman, dressed in a modest blue and white polka dot sundress, came to the door.

"Good morning. Is Mrs. Geist available?" Derek asked before Todd could do the honors.

"I'm Alma – one of the granddaughters," the woman said, holding out her hand with no sense of surprise at his stature. "You must be the private investigator."

"Derek DiLaurain," Todd interjected, holding himself taller with as much dignity as he could muster. Derek shook his head – if the kid was aiming that high, he was likely to be disappointed.

"Is that the Detective?!" an elderly but vivacious woman's voice called from inside.

"It is, Grandma!" Alma called back with a little too much volume. "She doesn't hear all that well," she whispered, turning back to Derek. "Try to talk a bit louder than normal."

"Will do," he said, and followed her into the suite.

It didn't take more than a glance to see that the rich traveled in significantly greater comfort than the hoi polloi. The room that stretched out before him must've been three times bigger than Derek's entire cabin. A stairway to the back left suggested more rooms — probably the bedroom, (or rooms), upstairs. Seated in an overstuffed leather easy chair next to a huge window that overlooked the ocean several stories below, was a petite older woman with coiffed white hair and alert blue eyes that quickly reminded him not to under-estimate her mental capacities, despite her obvious age. She wore a baggy sweat suit that Derek guessed probably cost more than his tuxedo. But the only obvious sign of her wealth and social status was a slightly gaudy, but undeniably beautiful turquoise bracelet.

"Nice bling," he commented, nodding at the intricate silverwork.

"Thank you. Designed it myself. It's Mr. DiLaurain, is it?" she asked, extending her hand without attempting to get up out of the chair.

"Mrs. Geist," Derek said, taking her hand while offering a business card. "I'm sorry to meet you under such... uncertain circumstances."

"I'm afraid you'll have to speak up a bit, young man. Hearing isn't what it used to be."

"I said, I'm sorry to meet you under such uncertain circumstances!" the PI repeated more forcefully.

"Ah, yes. Indeed," she said, drawing a deep breath and looking down with a worried frown. "'Uncertain' is an apt word. I just can't imagine where Arnold has gotten himself off to."

"Well we'll find him, ma'am. It's a big ship, but not so big that someone can disappear for very long." He was becoming increasingly convinced that wasn't the case, but he kept his opinions to himself. Part of him felt duplicitous for purposely misleading the old lady, but he had no intention of telling her – or anyone else – his premonitions. At least not until he had more to go on.

"I hope you're right, Mr. DiLaurain… So, this is the sort of thing you do on a regular basis – find lost people?"

"Sometimes. I've worked on a variety of cases."

"Some with Mr. Brady James, I'm told."

Derek nodded. Seemed everyone on the planet had heard of James. Not so many knew the name DiLaurain. "We've worked together on a number of cases, yes ma'am."

"Will you be consulting with him on this one?" He could hear the hopefulness in her voice.

"I will. As soon as I have enough information to outline my thoughts."

"Good. Good. So, what do you need to know?" He tried to ignore the relieved look on her face.

Derek started delicately, unwilling to push the worried wife too hard, too fast. She talked easily about how long she and her husband had been married, and how they enjoyed cruises, especially since Arnold had retired. Gradually, the PI got down to business.

"Your son Arnold is now the CEO of the Geist holding company?" he asked after leading up to it with a series of innocuous questions about the company and its evolution.

"He is. But, I'm sorry, how does this help you find Arnold?" Her piercing look told Derek that she had more than an inkling of where he was headed.

"Mrs. Geist, the ship's crew has searched for your husband for 12 hours now. I'm not saying that there's nowhere else onboard where he might be, but I need to consider other possibilities."

"Other possibilities?" She looked genuinely surprised, which surprised Derek.

"Well, yes. I learned long ago that it doesn't pay to ignore any possible explanations, no matter how unlikely they might be."

"You mean you think something bad might have happened to Grandpa?" Alma asked plaintively. Derek had nearly forgotten she was still in the cabin.

"He's just covering the bases," Todd interrupted. "We don't have any information that would suggest anything to the contrary. Isn't that right, Mr. DiLaurain?"

Derek played along with the company rep. If he wanted to play bigshot to the Geist granddaughter, it was no skin off his nose. "You got it. Just keeping an open mind."

"And exactly who *are* you?" the old woman asked the visibly cowed security flunky.

"Todd, Todd McMillan, ma'am. I work with the ship's security team."

"Hmmph. Well I would think that you both might spend more time trying to find where my husband might be hiding on this boat instead of making such irresponsible suggestions," Ida Geist fired back, her tone anything but hospitable.

"I'm not making any suggestions," the PI snapped, "just asking questions." He wasn't going to take that kind of crap from anyone, not even a worried old woman.

"I'm sure he's just doing his job, Granny," the wide-eyed granddaughter soothed.

"How much are they paying you, Mr. DiLaurain?" Mrs. Geist asked out of the blue.

"Grandma!" Alma interrupted.

The old lady waved her off like a buzzing fly. "This isn't a tea party, Alma," she said, looking Derek full in the face all the while, "this is business. And if I've learned one thing from spending all these years by Arnold's side, it's that money talks. Whatever they're paying you, I'll double it – IF you find my husband. Agreed?"

Derek tried to keep a poker face despite the potential windfall. "If the cruise company wouldn't mind…" he began.

"They won't. Isn't that right, Mr. McMillan?"

Todd swallowed. "I, ah, I really can't speak for the company, but I'm sure…"

"So am I," Mrs. Geist interrupted. "So, are we agreed?" she asked Derek.

"Agreed. But I do it my way, wherever that leads."

Ida looked as if she wanted to say something else, but apparently thought better of it. "Done. Now, if there's nothing else you need from me, I didn't get much sleep last night."

Derek recognized an oblique dismissal when he heard one. "All right, let's call it a day – for now. If I need more information from you…?"

"Talk to Alma. She'll make any arrangements that are needed."

"Okay then. First off, I'll need to talk to your sons."

A flicker of emotion that Derek couldn't quite place flickered across the old lady's face. "You'll have to arrange that with them directly," she said. "They've done pretty much whatever they please for a great many years."

"I'll do that." As he stood he nodded at Mrs. Geist. "Pleasant dreams."

"I doubt that, Mr. DiLaurain. I doubt that very much."

He chuckled inwardly at his off-handed insensitivity but doubted that the tough old bird in front of him would be severely wounded by his faux pas. Alma walked Todd and him to the door.

"You'll have to excuse her, Mr. DiLaurain. She's very upset."

"She seems a pretty strong woman."

"Oh, she's strong alright. *Had to be,* with Grandpa. But this whole episode has really shaken her. She's… more upset than I've ever seen her."

"Understandable, I suppose. By the way, Miss… Geist, is it?"

"It is, yes."

"Would you be available for a short interview?"

"Not right now. I need to help Granny get to bed. How about, say, in an hour or so?"

"Could you come down to the Security Office?"

"It's on B deck, near the Admin offices," Todd interjected, all too enthusiastically.

"I'm sure I'll find it. 11 work for you?"

"See you then."

As Derek and Todd left the cabin and made their way to the elevator, the young security assistant pumped the PI for any insights he could purloin and pass on to his boss as his own. He was so blatant that Derek couldn't resist playing with him a bit.

"So, you think Mr. Geist has fallen victim to foul play?" Todd asked with as much nonchalance as he could muster.

"*Fall victim? Foul play?* What is this, a Sherlock Holmes novel?"

The security man blushed. "I just meant…"

"I know what you meant," Derek sighed. It was too easy. "And the answer is yes, just between you and me – I think there's a pretty good chance something bad's happened to the old man. But you need to keep searching this boat to make sure he's not holed-up somewhere, or stuck in a service elevator, or asleep in the sauna, or whatever. Meanwhile, I'll talk to the rest of the family members and see if any of them have any ideas where he might be. And I'll contact my partner

Brady James back in the States and see if he can dig-up anything."

Todd stopped dead in his tracks. "You'll be working with Brady James?!" His awe made the PI queasy. "Wow. He's pretty much a legend in this business."

"Yeh, that's Brady all right," Derek said.

The young man pestered the PI with questions about James all the way back to the security offices. Derek gave him the CliffsNotes version: retired Washington Post crime reporter, recipient of the Pulitzer Prize, now a freelance 'consultant' on any kind of crazy criminal conundrum that the police – or anyone else who could get him interested – couldn't solve on their own. He tried to keep the irritation from his voice. It's not that he didn't like Brady, or even admire his investigative prowess. He was a good guy, and he did unravel a goodly number of difficult cases. But, damn it, he didn't do it by himself! Derek had worked with the great Mr. James from way back in his reporter days, and he had the scars to prove it. Derek had made some of the biggest discoveries in the cases that had made James a household name. But Derek DiLaurain? Nobody'd ever heard of him. One of these days he was going to work a case all by himself, just to show them all who needed who.

But maybe not this time.

By the time they got back to the security offices the little man was fuming.

"Any luck?" Ms. Earthal asked as soon as they came through the door.

She glanced up to see Todd motioning furiously from behind the PI's back to cut the questions.

"No, nothing yet," Derek growled as he stomped past her without so much as a glance in her direction. "But I'm about to contact Brady James, so I'm sure everything will be resolved before lunch."

Ms. Earthal snuck a glance at her assistant that suggested she hadn't missed the sarcasm.

"What's with him?" she whispered as Derek disappeared into the offices at the back of the suite.

"You got me. I asked him a few questions about Brady James, and he pulled an attitude."

"Anything useful from Ms. Geist?"

"Not really. She didn't seem to want to entertain the notion that her husband might have bigger problems than being lost. At least that's what Mr. DiLaurain thinks."

"Oh great," the security chief groaned. "That's all we need."

*****

"Brady, it's Derek," the PI said into the VoIP phone.

"Derek! What's up? Ship hit an iceberg?" Derek could hear a ballgame on the TV in the background.

"Nah, but they're running low on Dom Perignon – want to send over a case?"

"Sorry, bro. Down to my last few bottles. How's it goin'?"

"The cruise is fine, but they've got a little problem that I was hoping you might help me out with."

"What's that?"

"You've heard of Arnold Geist, the real estate guy?"

"Yeh, sure. He's got his name on half the new upscale developments from here to Timbuktu."

"That's him. Well, he was on this ship, but he's missing."

There was a short pause. "Missing? As in... what?"

"Don't know yet. But he was onboard with his entire family to celebrate his 90th birthday, and to announce the details of his will."

"Oh my. You mean the poor schmuck told his family members what they were going to get before he disappeared?"

"Maybe not so long before. He made the announcement last night, and a few hours later he turned up missing."

"You think he went for an unscheduled starlight swim?"

Derek smiled. James did have a way with words. "I'm starting to think it's a possibility, yeh."

"What do you want me to do?"

One thing about Brady, he didn't jerk you around. "Could you do some digging into his holding company – any financial problems, any in-house arguments, anything that might cause someone to hold a grudge?"

"Sure, I'll get on it this afternoon. Need me to come out there?"

Derek knew that Brady was just being supportive, just offering an honest helping hand. But something made him bridle at the suggestion. "No! Thanks, I don't think that's necessary quite yet. Maybe later."

"You're getting back at me for threatening to leave you home when we worked the fake swami case out in Vegas," James teased.

"Would serve you right. But if I need you, I'll call."

"All right. I'll keep a bag packed, just in case. Don't get too sunburned doing all those poolside interviews."

"I'll try. Say hi to Anne." Brady's better half was probably already on her way to the Senate office building where she worked as an 'office manager.'

"Will do. And Derek?"

"Yeh?"

"Take care. If a bigshot billionaire real estate tycoon can fall overboard, someone might wish the same on a smallshot thousandaire PI."

"I'll start wearing a life preserver under my shirt," Derek said with utter disdain. But as soon as he hung up he started to wonder if maybe James had been right. If someone *had* helped Geist over the side, one more accident wouldn't likely overwhelm their sense of guilt. He decided to keep away from the outer railings whenever he had to move around on-deck.

CHAPTER 4

Alma Geist was in her late twenties or early thirties, not much more than five feet tall, but she had inherited the good looks and lively blue eyes of her grandmother. Derek took one glance at the warm, inviting smile that greeted him when he answered her knock on the Security Office door, and wondered if she'd inherited the old lady's stiff backbone as well.

"Alma – thanks for coming down," he said as he stepped back to let her enter. "How's your grandmother doing?"

"Granny's tough, Mr. DiLaurain. But she seems pretty shook-up by all this uncertainty."

"I can imagine. Can I get you anything – coffee, a soda?" He'd asked the regular Security staff to take a break while he interviewed the granddaughter, thinking she might be more forthcoming if it was just *little ol'* Derek and her.

"I wouldn't mind a glass of water." She glanced around at the elegantly furnished office. "You have a nice work environment here."

"Not mine," he said as he filled a glass with water from a cooler in the corner. "I'm just a passenger on this ship, like you."

"Oh? How did you get involved in all this?" Apparently the family elders hadn't shared all the particulars of his recruitment with her.

Derek wasn't used to being the one interviewed, but decided to set an example. "The ship's security chief somehow found out that I've done a considerable amount of work with an old Washington Post writer by the name of Brady James," he began, handing the young woman the glass.

"So I understand," she said. "Grandma was terribly impressed."

Derek tried not to grimace. "Yes, well, we have had some luck in a few high-profile cases."

"Like when that guy wanted to blow up the President out in Vegas?"

"Ah, so you know about that one, huh?"

"It was on all the news. Were you out in Vegas when they caught the guy?"

The PI's eyes narrowed. *He'd* been the one to actually put the kid out of commission. "Yeh, I was there. But what do you say we chat a bit about your grandfather, and some of the other members of your family. You're Arnold Jr's daughter, is that right?"

Alma's expression became noticeably more serious. "I am, yes. I have two siblings."

"The other two – brothers?"

She shook her head. "Alexandra is the oldest, and then Arnie."

"Your family seems to have something of a love affair with names that begin with *A*," Derek said.

Alma laughed, a sweet, gentle sound that made Derek instantly take a liking to her. That, despite the fact that she was filthy rich.

"It all goes back to grandfather," she explained between sips of water. "He wanted his first son named after him, but when Alex came along he insisted that *at least* the child's name begin with an *A*. After that, it sort of snowballed."

Derek thought he detected the slightest hint of disapproval from the big man's granddaughter.

"What's he like – your grandfather?" he pursued. He almost put the old man in the past tense, but caught himself.

"Grandfather?" The young woman stopped and pursed her lips as if considering exactly how to answer. She blinked several times. "He's a very... determined man. He built his fortune all by himself – didn't inherit a thing from his father." Derek knew all that; it was part of Geist's standard bio. But he decided to let her tell the tale in her own good time. 'A little patience goes a long ways', Brady always said. He'd try to stay patient.

"And," Alma went on after a short hesitation, "I suppose he always put his business ahead of everything else. I mean, there are only so many hours in the day."

Derek followed-up immediately. "So he wasn't around much as his kids were growing up?"

"I wasn't there," she said with a winsome smile, "but from the stories I've heard it was Grandma who did most of the child-raising. The home was her domain, the office was his."

"And later on, when you were growing up – did you see much of him then?"

A hard-to-define look was quickly dispatched. "Sometimes. Not so much," she fumbled. "You've got to understand – he was still going to the office every day until he turned 75, and he didn't turn over the reins to Daddy until about five years ago."

"What did your father think about that? I mean, was he anxious to run the show by himself?"

"Well, there's a Board of Directors you know." She sounded defensive.

"But the CEO calls the shots in most companies. Was your father getting antsy waiting for his father to finally fade into the sunset?"

She bobbed her head to and fro as if weighing her answer. "Daddy knew how important the business was to grandfather, so he understood, but I guess he was pretty much ready to take over, yeh."

"And since Arnold Sr. retired – has he kept out of the company business, or does he like to dip his fingers back into the waters every now and then?" Derek tried to sound casual, but Alma picked up on the undercurrent.

"Do you mean do he and Daddy ever have disagreements? I suppose so. I'm not really part of all that."

The PI felt Alma beginning to close-up and decided to switch tracks. "Okay. I'll ask your Dad about that. How about your uncle, Ayden? What kind of a guy is he?"

She lifted her hands in amused surrender. "Uncle Ayden? Hard to say. I'm not sure anyone outside his immediate family knows him well. He's very quiet."

"But a good guy?"

"He's always been good to me."

"Did he get along with your grandfather?"

A look of bewilderment crept over her. "Why are you asking? I mean, you don't think that Uncle Ayden, or Daddy, have done anything to hurt Grandfather, do you?"

Derek suddenly realized that he'd lapsed into past tense. "No! I'm just trying to get a picture of how everyone fits into the family portrait, if you know what I mean." He didn't particularly like to lie, but he certainly couldn't tell the complete truth without risking alienating the girl.

The lie seemed to work. Alma's shoulders relaxed noticeably. "Well, I guess they got along pretty well. As well as they could. I mean, Grandfather was always at the office, and Uncle Ayden was always sort of off in his own world, so I don't really know how they got along. You should ask them."

"I will. How about the youngest brother – Aaron was it?"

"Uncle Aaron is 180 degrees different than Uncle Ayden. He's funny, outgoing, easy to talk to."

"Do you talk to him a lot?"

"Sometimes. I know I can always pick up the phone and call him if I have a problem."

"And your grandfather? How do those two get along?"

This time the hesitation was more marked. "Okay, I guess."

"I'm only asking, because last night I happened to see your family in the ship's dining room, and I think it was your Uncle Aaron who was having a lively 'discussion' with your grandfather."

"They didn't mean anything by it!" Alma said defensively. "People in our family always speak their minds."

"And what was Aaron speaking his mind about then?"

"He… wasn't happy about the will," she said with visible reluctance.

"Your grandfather's will?"

"Yeh. Grandfather read it to everyone after dinner. Several folks weren't happy."

"Aaron and who else? You?"

"No!" she fired back. "I was actually very happy. Surprised even. Uncle Aaron and Daddy were not so pleased."

"Were they cut out of the will?" If they were, that certainly could've caused the brouhaha he'd witnessed at dinner time.

Alma smiled and shook her head. "Of course not. But they expected more, I guess."

"Would I be snooping if I asked how much they did get?"

She pressed her lips together as if torn. "I really don't know if I should be telling the family's secrets."

"How about in general? A few million, tens of millions, hundreds of millions…"

"Tens of millions I think would be about right."

"Nothing to sneeze at."

"No, but when you're talking about billions, I guess it seemed kind of *ungracious*." Something about the way she said the word raised Derek's antennae.

"Is that what your uncle called it – ungracious?"

"No. My Dad. I mean, he runs the holding company. He's been responsible for generating more than half the company's current net worth. I think he expected something more... commensurate with his contributions." The PI was pretty sure that was another quote from her father.

"And Aaron? Same thing?"

"Uncle Aaron?" She made a comical face. "I doubt he's contributed a dime to the net worth of the company in his whole life." She leaned in toward Derek and lowered her voice. "He's the black sheep of the family, you know."

"So did your father get a lot more than your uncle?" At this point he was fishing for any motive for whatever might have befallen the old man.

"That was the whole point," she went on, leaning back in her chair. "All three brothers got exactly the same."

"Was Ayden okay with that?"

"Uncle Ayden never complains about anything, at least not that I hear. He's always very level, very calm." Derek remembered the old saying about still waters.

"And how about the grandkids – did they all get the same as each other?"

For just an instant Alma's face froze, her eyes wary. "No, not really," she finally said softly.

"Oh? Who was the big winner?"

"All of us were *very* well taken care of," she defended.

'The lady doth protest too much,' he thought. "Including you? How did you do, relative to your cousins?"

"Very well. I did well." She seemed flustered.

"How well? As well as your uncles and father?"

More hesitation before a rapid-fire admission. "Actually, better. But I was always his favorite."

Interesting. "And your grandmother? Did she inherit the bulk of the estate?"

"Well, I don't know if it was the *bulk*, but she got a good bit, yes."

"Did she seem pleased? Or maybe she already knew about all the arrangements in advance."

"I don't think so. But like I already told you, Grandma is a pretty strong woman. She almost never shows her feelings. Although…"

"What?" Derek tried not to pounce too eagerly.

"Well, there were a few times she seemed genuinely surprised. But whether it was good surprised or bad surprised, I couldn't tell you."

"Do you remember when by any chance?"

"Not really. Only that I saw her eyes open a smidge wider than usual a couple of times."

Derek made a mental note to follow-up with the others.

"That's about all the questions I have for now," he said as he began to close up his notebook. "Oh, one more," he added as the thought popped into his mind. "Do you have *any* idea where your grandfather might be, or who I should talk to – aside from your immediate family?"

"I don't know. It's all so terrible. Being the last one to have seen him before he disappeared…"

Derek interrupted her. "How's that? I would've thought your grandmother, or his nurse would've been the last."

"Didn't anyone tell you? I took Grandfather on a walk, up on deck, around… midnight or so. He was still boiling about my uncles' 'insufferable thanklessness' I think he called it."

"So what – he asked you to take him out for some air?"

"He did. Grandma doesn't have the strength to push him anymore, and the nurse had already gone to bed."

"You were still awake?"

"I'm a bit of a night-owl."

"What did you talk about?"

"Not so much, really. At first he was complaining about my uncles, but then he just got quiet and stared out at the sea and sky. Just thinking, I imagine."

"How long were you up there?"

"I don't know. Maybe a half-hour or so? It was getting a bit cool for him, so I took him back to the cabin."

"And as far as you know, he didn't see or speak to anyone after you returned?"

A short but shaky pause. "After? Not that I know of. But have you spoken to his nurse? He calls her at all hours."

"That was..." Derek reopened the notebook and began to flip through the pages.

"Dalisay. She's Filipina."

"Know where she is by any chance?"

"Not right this second. But her cabin is down on D deck. 1266, I think."

"She doesn't have a cabin up on this deck?"

"No, but she has a cot in Grandfather's cabin whenever there's the need."

"Must get crowded in there with your grand-mother, grandfather and his nurse."

Alma smiled wanly. "They don't *sleep* together," she explained. "Haven't for years now. Even before Grandfather got stuck in the wheelchair, Grandma said he snored like a chainsaw."

"How does your grandmother get along with this Dalisay? I would think it'd be difficult: two women looking after one guy."

The young woman lifted an eyebrow. "Okay, I guess. Dalisay does most of the looking after at this point."

"I see. Okay, thanks for the info. Can I give you a call if I need anything else?"

"Of course. Anything I can do, just let me know."

"I'll do that," the PI said, standing up to show the granddaughter to the door.

"And Mr. DiLaurain?"

"Yes?"

"Find him. Please. I'd rather have Grandfather back than any amount of money."

Despite her seeming sincerity, Derek had his doubts. In his experience when it came to money, *real* money, family often took a back seat.

*****

Dalisay Cruz was just where Alma had suggested: in her cabin down on D deck. Derek didn't bother to clear the visit with Arnold Jr., or Mrs. Geist, but then again she'd hired him so why ask?

He knocked loudly on the metal door.

The woman who answered was a tall, thin, positively beautiful young woman with olive skin, dark hair and eyes, dressed in a tailored business suit that looked like it came from Park Ave.

"Ms. Cruz?" he asked, taken aback.

"You are Mr. DiLaurain?" she asked, her English slightly accented with the quasi-Spanish lilt of so many Filipinas.

"I am. Thank you for meeting with me."

"Of course, of course. All this is so terrible. Come in."

The D level cabin was virtually identical to Derek's, perhaps even a little smaller. Somehow it didn't seem sufficiently grand for this... nurse.

"May I get you something – a cup of tea or coffee?" she asked as she showed him to the sole chair in the room.

"No, I'm good, thanks," he said, trying to position himself in the easy chair so as not to appear too ridiculous with his legs dangling in mid-air. He was only partly successful.

She, on the other hand, settled gracefully on the edge of the bed.

"Have you found anything more about Mr. Geist?" she asked as she smoothed her skirt. "This is too terrible."

"Not yet, I'm afraid. But we're working on it. May I ask you a few questions?"

"Of course."

"Have you worked for Mr. Geist for a long time?"

"Eleven years. I started just two years after I graduated from nursing school in Manila."

"Manila? That's a long ways from the U.S. How did Mr. Geist ever find you?"

"A friend of his, a business man named Harvey Singleton, suffered a small stroke while visiting Manila. I was hired to help him recover, and he recommended me to Mr. Geist."

"Did you know who Mr. Geist was back then?"

"No," she said with a smile and a shake of her head. "Just a friend of Mr. Singleton's who needed some help."

"Was it difficult getting to the U.S.? I mean, with visas, work permits, and all that?"

"Oh no! Mr. Geist took care of all that. Or actually, some people at his company did." The nurse seemed perfectly poised. No sign of nervousness, or worry for that matter.

"What is he like – Mr. Geist?"

"Mr. Geist…" It was clear she was weighing her words. "Is a very successful businessman."

"Yes, I know, but how is he to work for? Is he kind? Demanding? Grouchy?"

Ms. Cruz tilted her head side to side as the weighing continued. "He can be demanding, yes. But he is a very fair man. If you do as he asks, he is kind in return."

"And if you don't? If you make a mistake?"

Her smile seemed forced. "He is very demanding."

"I bet," he said off-handedly. "Last night, did you accompany Mr. Geist to the big family dinner up in the dining room?"

"I did. I go pretty much everywhere with him. He uses a wheelchair, you know."

"Yes, of course. So, last night, it seems things got a little heated with some of the family members."

"Some of them were not pleased, yes."

"Any idea why? Did Mr. Geist mention anything after the dinner?"

Ms. Cruz straightened. "I do not repeat what Mr. Geist has said in confidence."

"No! Of course not, and in normal circumstances I'd applaud that stance. But your boss is missing – disappeared into thin air. It's possible that something he said to you, or that you overheard, might help us find him."

He watched her wrestle with his words. "Yes, I see... All right. He did mention something – only it was before the dinner."

"Oh? And what was that?"

"Well, he said that his children were not going to be happy despite the large amounts of money that he was leaving them in his will."

Derek leaned forward, his interest suddenly piqued. "What did he say, exactly?"

She blushed. "People sometimes say things when they're upset, or when they're very old."

'And old man Geist had both of those going for him,' Derek thought. "I understand completely," he said. "But it might be important. Can you remember *exactly* what he said?"

She took a deep breath. "He said 'my kids aren't going to be happy tonight after they hear my will – greedy little bastards that they are.'" The nurse looked down at her folded hands.

"Anything else? Did he mention any of the kids in particular?"

"No, not in particular. But he did tell me, 'Watch your back. When they find out what I'm leaving you, they're going to go… bat-shit.'"

"But he didn't warn you against any one of them specifically?" The PI knew that such a direct accusatory statement would be unlikely, but it was worth asking.

"No, I don't think so."

"How much?" he asked. "How much did he leave you?"

The young woman looked back down at her hands and her blush deepened two shades. "Quite a lot," she said softly.

"Could you be a little more specific?"

She paused so long that Derek was about to give her another little shove, when she finally found her voice. "Twenty-five million," she whispered.

"TWENTY-FIVE MILLION DOLLARS!" Derek exploded. He'd been thinking something in the vicinity of a mil or so. Twenty-five was enough to piss any kid off – or anyone else who thought they deserved a piece of the pie.

Dalisay suddenly roared back to life. "He said it was because I'd shown him more simple human kindness than anyone in his family!" she explained forcefully. "He said I was more like a child to him than any of his real children."

Derek nodded thoughtfully. "Okay, I guess I can see that. And for him, $25 million wasn't really all that much. How did the kids take it?"

Her face twisted into an unrestrained mask of distaste. "Aaron started yelling and screaming that his father had lost his mind. Said he was going to talk to a lawyer."

"And the others?"

"Arnold Junior tried to calm his brother, but said he wasn't too sure of his father's competency either."

"Ayden?"

"Mr. Ayden never says much. He just sort of tipped his head."

"Any of the others show a reaction?"

"Well, I guess all of them looked a little surprised. Except Mr. Geist himself. He laughed out loud."

"I bet that went over well."

"I thought Mr. Aaron was going to throw something at him. And Mr. Arnold turned all red in the face."

Hmm. Two kids ticked-off. Maybe in cahoots?

"What happened then? After all the shouting, I mean."

"Mr. Arnold Jr. and Mr. Aaron left the room very angry, with Mrs. Arnold Jr. and their children close behind."

"Including Alma?" The PI suddenly wondered why the granddaughter had failed to mention that little detail.

"Miss Alma? Let me think… No, no she stayed behind. Miss Alma was always Mr. Geist's favorite."

"Okay. So Arnold Junior and his family and Ayden all walked out. What happened then?"

"Not so much. Mr. Geist told everyone to enjoy themselves – and each other, since the next day we would be in Bermuda and they'd probably all go their separate ways. And then he finished his dessert."

"Did everyone else hang around?"

"Until Mr. Geist finished eating, yes. Then he shooed them all away, and we went back to their cabin."

"With Mrs. Geist?"

"Yes, of course."

"What time was that?"

"Oh, around 9 p.m. I'd say."

"And then what?"

"Well, I got Mr. Geist comfortably situated back in his cabin, and then he dismissed me and said he'd call when he was ready for bed."

"Is that how it usually went? He'd lounge around a bit and then give you a call to get him into bed?"

"Usually, yes. Mrs. Geist can no longer help him from his wheelchair to the bed, so one of them usually calls when he's ready."

"And when did he call?"

"That's the whole point!" she said, her voice rising in pitch and volume. "He never called! I waited until almost midnight, and then just lay down to rest my eyes for a moment, and the next thing I knew the ship's security people were banging on my door in the middle of the night."

"So you never saw him again after you brought him back to the cabin after dinner?"

"Never. Do you think something bad has happened?"

"I don't know. At this point it's all just guesswork, but it's more than a little strange that the ship's crew can't find him. I mean, this is a big boat, but the guy's 90 and in a wheelchair. Unless he somehow got in the wrong room and slept-in, I've got to consider the possibility that something happened to him."

She shook her head and looked down at her hands. "I hope you're wrong."

Derek thought about feeding her a reassuring line, but then reconsidered.

"So do I, Miss Cruz. So do I."

CHAPTER 5

The nurse wasn't able to provide any further information to advance his investigation, so Derek went in search of the three Geist sons. His search was a short one.

"Oh, I think they've left the ship," Miss Earthal said when he asked her where he might find them.

"Their father's still missing, and they left the ship?" The PI was getting the distinct feeling that the sons weren't enamored of their bigshot father.

"Perhaps they had things to do."

"Did they say what kinds of things?"

"We are not in the habit of interrogating our guests," the Security Chief said with disdain.

"But you're not in the habit of losing guests either – at least I assume you're not."

"Of course not! This is the first such incident we have had in… years."

"That's reassuring. Any idea how I can track the three caballeros?"

"You might ask the taxi drivers."

"And how would I find them?"

"Check with the purser's office. Their people record all the license plates of the taxis that pick up our passengers."

"I'll do that. Where do I find him?"

"*Her* office is just down the hall. But I doubt she's there, now that we're in port."

"Where is she likely to be?"

"Try the gangway. She's probably keeping an eye on the disembarkation."

"Thanks. I'll do that."

Derek made his way down to the deck where the ship's gangway extended out to the Bermuda Dockside landing. There was an excited huddle of passengers waiting patiently to set foot on the tiny island, exchanging tour tips and restaurant reviews as hundreds of their fellow travelers crowded the deck on either side of the narrow exit ramp. The PI had to force his way through the bottleneck, eliciting more than one surprised gasp as his head passed at barely waist-level. Finally he made his way to where some officious looking Princess staffers stood checking names against a clipboard list.

"Name?" the woman in charge asked without even looking up from her list.

"DiLaurain. Derek DiLaurain," the PI said loudly enough to be heard over the babble of voices.

"Just yourself?" the woman asked, glancing down at him for the first time.

"I'm not looking to leave the boat – not yet," he explained. "I just need some information."

"We are very busy here just now, Mr. DiLaurain. If you can wait an hour or so until we've completed our disembarkation…"

"I've been hired to locate Mr. Geist," he said. The woman's eyes widened and she glanced quickly from side to side.

"Oh! Of course." She turned to a younger woman standing next to her wearing the omnipresent Princess blue blazer. "Jackie – can you take care of the list while I speak with this gentleman?"

She passed the clipboard to her associate before she could answer.

"Would you please follow me?" she said to Derek, and then threaded her way expertly through the mass of people to a nearby deck lounge. Derek followed in her wake. The purser made sure they were alone before closing the door.

"So they still haven't found him?" she asked before Derek could say a word.

"Not yet. Miss…?"

"Lansky. Audrey Lansky," she said, holding out her hand. "I don't believe we've met. Are you part of the security team?"

"Private investigator. Just happened to be on the ship."

"Oh. Well that's a lucky coincidence. How can I help you, Mr. DiLaurain?"

He studied her closely for just a moment: tall, thin, late 30's-early 40's, bleached blond hair. The thin lips and hard mouth that in his experience usually signified an unmarried, work-obsessed professional woman. "I've been told by your Ms. Earthal in Security that Mr. Geist's sons left the ship earlier this morning. Is that right?"

"I believe that Arnold Jr. and his family left quite early. Aaron maybe an hour ago. I don't know about the middle one. Why?"

"Oh, I'm just interviewing everyone who might have seen Mr. Geist Sr. last night. Routine in this kind of thing. Do you happen to know where they went – Arnold Jr and Aaron?"

"If I remember correctly, Mr. Arnold said they were going to the Coral Queen. I don't think Mr. Aaron said."

"Is there any way to find out – where Aaron went?"

"Well, we could check with the taxi driver…"

"Would you? I'd appreciate it." He smiled his most winning smile.

"I think we might be able to track him down. Let me check with Jackie."

Five minutes later, the purser's assistant had contacted the driver by cellphone and had located the youngest of the Geist brothers. He was staying at The Hibiscus. Derek thanked both Ms. Lansky and Jackie before heading to Ayden Geist's suite to see if the middle brother was still onboard.

His knock was answered almost immediately by a five or six year old girl, her fiery red hair pulled up in pigtails, freckles surrounding pale green eyes.

"Well hello there," he said as warmly as if he actually liked kids. "What's your name?"

"I'm not supposed to talk to strangers," the girl said.

"That's a good rule to follow. Is your grandfather home?"

"Who is calling?" she asked.

"Derek DiLaurain. Tell him it's about his father."

The girl turned back into the cabin. "Grandpa, a little man named Derek wants to talk to you about Great-Grandpa!" she screamed so loudly she could probably be heard ten cabins away. "He's coming," she said to Derek a few second later.

"Thanks."

The girl eyed him up and down as they waited for her grandfather. "You know, you're not very tall," she finally said.

"So I've been told," Derek answered, this time making no effort to sound warm and cuddly.

"Why?"

"Why what? Why am I so short?"

The girl nodded.

"I smoked too many cigarettes when I was your age and didn't eat my Brussel sprouts."

"I don't like Brussel sprouts."

"Watch out. You may end up as short as me."

Her eyes grew wide.

Just then the door opened wide and Ayden Geist stepped forward.

"You're the private investigator that Mother engaged?" he asked without so much as a 'good morning'.

"I am. Derek DiLaurain," the tiny PI said, reaching up to offer his hand.

The middle Geist son ignored the gesture and turned back toward his cabin. "I suppose we should talk," he muttered over his shoulder. "Otherwise I'll have to listen to Mother complaining all day."

"You seem more worried about her than your father," Derek said as he followed Ayden into the suite of rooms, giving the little girl an exaggerated stink-eye as he passed.

"You don't know him. He might've decided he wanted some guava ice cream and jumped ship right after dinner without telling anyone – other than the nurse, of course."

"Is that something he might do?"

"I wouldn't be all that surprised. I think he's losing it in a big way," he added, winding his finger in a circle beside his right ear.

"Dementia?"

"Or Alzheimer's. Something. Of course I'm just guessing. We'd be the last to know."

"Ayden, you mustn't say such things!" a very attractive woman a good twenty years younger than the Geist brother said as she strolled into the room. "He'll think you're serious!"

"I *am* serious!" her husband barked with no sign of amusement. "And you know it."

The woman, dressed in a fashionable blue pinstripe suit that would look more at home in a boardroom than on a cruise ship, came over to Derek with her hand extended.

"Eileen. Eileen Geist," she introduced herself.

The woman bent down to eye level and stared into his eyes with such vehemence that he backed up half a step.

"Derek DiLaurain – private investigator," he managed to spit out.

"Ah yes. You're trying to locate Arnold Sr., aren't you?"

"I am. Know where he is?" DiLaurain asked, growing tired of the whole, dysfunctional family.

"Is that meant to be a joke?" Ayden asked sharply.

"Yes and no. Nobody seems to know anything about your father's disappearance, and not many of you seem to care a whole lot."

"I wouldn't say that!" Eileen protested.

"I would," her husband countered. "The Old Man's always been a big pain in the ass, and he hasn't been getting any easier to get along with recently."

"You mean the reading of the will?" Derek asked with practiced innocence.

"You know about that, huh? Who's been bending your ear – Arnie?"

"More likely Aaron," Eileen interjected, all pretense of kumbaya thrown out the porthole.

"Actually, I haven't had the pleasure of speaking with either of your brothers – yet," Derek said. "Seems they both left the boat earlier this morning."

"Not surprised," Ayden said. "Arnie's grandkids were going a little stir-crazy onboard this tub, and Aaron, well, he's probably ensconced in some Tiki bar, or the Bermuda equivalent, by now."

"None of you think that anything bad might have happened to Arnold Sr?"

"The man is 90 years old. You've heard how cats have nine lives? He must have ninety-nine."

"Can I ask you where you were last night after dinner?"

Ayden hesitated, staring at Derek as if he'd just smelled a noxious gaseous release. "This is starting to sound like a scene from Dragnet."

Eileen chuckled. "You're dating yourself, Ayden. Nowadays it's more like CSI."

"Whatever. Why the third degree? You think something happened to the Old Man?"

"I really don't know. But I've got to track down every possibility until we know for sure. So – last night?"

Ayden flopped down into a leather armchair and leaned back with an exasperated shake of his head.

"What a mess," he said wearily. "It was almost as if Dad *wanted* to stir things up."

Eileen motioned for Derek to sit on a sofa that faced Ayden's chair. "Before you two get into this, can I get you anything?"

"Is it too early for a beer?" the PI asked.

"It's your liver."

"If it's not ruined yet, it'll never be. Anything cold would be great. Thanks."

As she left, Derek scooted up on the sofa. No matter how he situated himself, however, his legs dangled inauspiciously in thin air.

"They always make these things too damn tall," he muttered.

"If you'd be more comfortable somewhere else…" Ayden offered.

"Nah. Same problem everywhere. So, you were saying about the dinner – how your father seemed to want to stir things up?"

"If he wanted us to know the details of his will, he could've called my brothers and me into his office, or sent us letters, or… I don't know. But he didn't need to make such a big show out of it. With all the kids around, onboard the ship."

"So you were angry with him?"

"We were *all* angry with him. Most of the time lately, actually. If he were a kid I'd say he was going through 'a phase'."

"I don't mean to be rude, but did you get what you expected? I mean, did your father take good care of you in the will?"

He shrugged. "So-so. I mean, it's not as if we *need* all that money. None of us. But if he's going to give $25 million to his nurse, for God's sake…"

"That was unexpected?"

"Not the gift. We all expected he'd leave her something. I mean, she's been with him virtually 24 hours a day for years now. She deserves something. But $25 million? That's a lot of sponge baths."

"Are you suggesting there was more to their relationship than patient–nurse?"

"I don't know. I wouldn't put it past him. But *she* seems pretty straightforward." He stared out the sliding glass door at the palm trees blowing in the breeze. "No, on second thought, it's probably just sour grapes. Maybe he just wanted to tweak the rest of us. Especially Aaron."

"Why Aaron? Do your father and he not get along?"

Just then his wife returned with a Coors Light and a tall glass on a small tray. "Hope Coors will do," she said, setting the tray down on the coffee table in front of him.

"Beggars can't be choosers," he said, before pouring the beer into the glass and taking a long, slow quaff that emptied fully half its contents. "Ahhh. Thanks." He wiped away a foamy mustache with the back of his hand.

"You're welcome. Can I get you two anything else?"

"Not for me," Derek said.

"No, thanks honey. I'm fine."

"Then, if you'll excuse me, I'm in the middle of a good murder mystery and I want to go find out 'who done it'."

Ayden watched her leave until the door to the adjacent room swung shut, when he turned his attention back to the PI.

"You were asking?"

"About Aaron – doesn't he get along with your father?"

"Never has. Ever since he was a little kid, Aaron has been... different. He's always been happy-go-lucky, at least as long as the folks pick up the tab."

"And your father doesn't like that?"

"Ha. My father was born the second of five children of a shoe salesman in Columbus, Ohio. He made every penny of his fortune himself – at least until Arnie and I came onboard. He's always expected us boys to live up to that standard. Aaron never had much interest."

"Do they quarrel?"

"Did Custer and Sitting Bull quarrel? Dad and Aaron are as different as different can be. Sometimes we wonder if he's even our biological brother."

Derek's eyebrow shot up in spite of himself. "Literally?"

Ayden smiled sheepishly. "Nah. You can take one look at him and see our mother in his face. Not so much Dad, but enough so there was never a need for a DNA test."

Derek struggled to think of a diplomatic way to ask the next question. "Was there ever… another man?"

"With Mom?" he asked, his surprise undisguised. "I don't think so. But, now that you mention it, I can't say for sure. Dad was gone a lot of the time."

Another note jotted down. "But never any arguments? Accusations?"

"Not that I heard. But I haven't lived with them for 45 years."

"And how about your brothers – do they get along with their father?"

Derek couldn't tell if the twist to Ayden's mouth was a sneer or a smirk.

"From time to time. Arnie is probably too much like the Old Man, and Aaron not like him enough. Causes friction from time to time."

"Any recently?"

"You mean, was anyone mad enough to do him harm? Nah, I don't think so. Oh, they'll both stomp their feet and shout when they don't get their way, but I don't think they'd hurt Dad."

"Any of the other family members? Grandkids, maybe?"

"I really don't think anyone in the family would hurt Dad."

"How about outside? Anyone he works with or interacts with outside the immediate family?"

"Look, Mr. DiLaurain, my father has been a big-time businessman for a long time. You can't do that as long as he has and not make a few enemies."

"Any in particular?"

"Not that I know of. You should ask Arnie. Or maybe Mom."

Derek held his pen above the notebook, poised for some final notes. "Anything else? Anything that might help us find him?"

The middle son shook his head slowly. "Not really. I've been trying to figure out where he might be, just like everyone else, but I'm afraid I don't have a clue."

"Hmm," the PI said as he put away his notebook and handed Ayden a business card. "If you get any ideas, or hear from him, would you give me a call?"

"Sure. But you'd probably be better off talking to Arnie and Aaron. I think they communicate more with him than I do."

"I plan to. As soon as I can get ahold of them." He picked up his beer glass from the side table and drained the last of the warm Coors Lite. "Thanks for your time."

Ayden pushed himself up out of his chair with a low groan and saw Derek to the door.

"Do you really think something's happened to him?" he asked with much less attitude as they stood in the doorway shaking hands.

"Starting to look that way. But who knows? Maybe's he's just eating that ice cream you mentioned."

"Maybe."

Derek turned to leave before a thought stopped him in mid-stride even as the door to the cabin began to swing shut behind him.

"Oh, one other thing," he said, turning back toward Ayden. "If you and your brothers, and the nurse, all get relatively small pieces of the pie, who gets the rest? Your mother?"

"She, and his Foundation – which she and Arnie effectively run."

"So she's well taken care of."

"Very."

"Right. Well, thanks again. And thank your wife for the beer."

As the door began to shut again, Derek heard the young granddaughter calling out from just inside the cabin. "Grandpa, I'm going to eat all my Brussel sprouts from now on!"

"Glad I accomplished *something*," the PI said to himself as he waddled down the hallway.

*****

"I will go with you." Olga stood watching Derek load some gear into his backpack.

"It's not going to be much fun, I'm afraid. I've gotta go find the two brothers and see what they have to say."

"Better than sit all day, or lay by pool and listen to little children yell at top of lungs."

He nodded agreeably. "You may have a point there. Alright, but I wanna be off this boat in no more than a half-hour."

"I will be ready," she said, and went immediately to prepare.

Derek flipped on the television and was watching some promo produced by the Bermuda Tourist Bureau when a knock sounded at his door.

"Now what?" Derek grumbled as he went to answer it.

Ms. Earthal was standing at the door accompanied by what the PI assumed – from the uniform – was a Bermuda police official.

"Mr. DiLaurain – can we chat for a moment? We have news," the security chief said. From her expression Derek assumed it wasn't good news.

"Yeh, sure, come in."

"This is Bermuda Chief Inspector Bradley Trott," Caroline introduced as she slid past Derek.

The two men shook hands and exchanged pleasantries.

"Do I take it you've turned up something about Mr. Geist?" Derek asked as he motioned for them to take a seat.

"Chief Inspector?" the ship's security chief deferred.

Trott was a tall, sturdy black man, with the creamy coffee skin tone so common to many of the islanders. He wore a brilliant white dress uniform that Derek assumed was worn in deference to the missing high-ranking visitor.

"A tourist found Mr. Geist's hat, washed up on the beach at Spanish Point," he explained without introduction. "Found it about an hour ago, just by chance. Was out taking a walk."

"A hat? How can you be sure it was Geist's?" the PI asked.

"Had his name stitched inside the band," Ms. Earthal cut in. "When we showed it to Mrs. Geist she identified it immediately. Seems it was custom made for her husband."

Although the news was not unexpected, it hit Derek hard. Even after all the years he'd been mixed up in that crazy business, he still hated to hear about senseless deaths. "So... you think he went overboard?"

"Might have," the Inspector said. "Then again, someone might have tossed it overboard to make us think he had, or maybe it just blew off his head. No way to tell at this point."

Derek nodded, duly impressed. The cop had an open mind. Good. "You've got people out sweeping the Bay?"

"We've got a couple of cutters out there, with divers. But odds are that the body – if there is a body," he quickly corrected himself, "is probably outside the reef."

"Is the water deep?"

"Not so deep close-in, but it falls off fairly rapidly."

"Currents?"

"Some."

"Do you have someone who can track the ocean movements from where the Princess was last night around midnight?"

"We're working on it. We've got some of our own people, plus there's been a team from California State University – Monterey Bay out here doing some charting of the ocean floor and deep water caves. We're trying to get them involved as well."

"So what's the status of the investigation?"

"We're still treating this as a missing person, until and unless we have some reason to think otherwise."

"It'd be pretty hard for a wheelchair-bound 90 year old to accidentally fall overboard, wouldn't it?"

The Inspector glanced over at Ms. Earthal. "Hard, but not impossible," he said.

"So that's how you want it handled as the investigation continues?" the PI asked.

"If you're discussing the case with anyone, yes. But of course, we'd prefer to keep this close-hold until we know something further."

Derek knew what the security chief meant was that her front office had told her to keep a lid on it until they absolutely couldn't keep the disappearance a secret any longer. Something like this – a billionaire disappearing from one of their Bermuda cruises – would be bad for business. Maybe real bad.

"Understood," he said. "I'm about to head out to track down Arnold Jr. and his youngest brother. Anything I need to know?"

"Nothing from us," Earthal said. "Inspector?"

"Not that I need to remind you," the local cop said with perhaps a bit too much emphasis, "but you aren't licensed in Bermuda. Any investigation you undertake will be just as a private citizen. We do not tolerate interference in our inquiries. And, of course, no weapons."

"Of course not!" Derek said, fingering the switchblade he always carried in his front pants pocket.

"I'm only going to ask a few questions. See if I can get some idea what happened out there."

"You *will* share that information with the Bermuda Police Department." It was a statement, not a question.

"Actually, I'll share it with Ms. Earthal and Mrs. Geist, who are my clients. I'm sure *they* will share it with you as appropriate." Derek couldn't resist tweaking cops who lorded their authority over him. Even if this particular Inspector smiled and spoke with a winning Bermudian lilt.

"We will keep you informed," Ms. Earthal said.

The Inspector bobbed his head in her direction. Derek thought he detected a hint of a sneer in his.

"If that's all, I'd better be getting on my way," the PI announced when a long silence suggested the meeting was over.

"Take care out there," the security chief said.

"What – on the mean streets of Hamilton?"

"*If* Mr. Geist went overboard," the Inspector explained with strained patience, "then we must assume that someone *helped* him. That someone is still at large."

"I take your point. I'll keep my eyes open."

"You do that."

As he closed the door behind his departing guests, Derek hoped he wouldn't need too much help from the local cops. If the Inspector were any indication, he wouldn't be getting it.

*****

Olga emerged from the bathroom looking as if she were ready for an afternoon soiree: makeup perfectly arranged, hair coiffed, a powder blue silk blouse over three-quarter length white Capris, Louis Vuitton pumps, topped off by a broad-brimmed straw hat and designer sunglasses.

"I'm going to interview two guys about a possible homicide," he said when she modeled the look in front of him, "not to Churchill Downs."

She pouted. "Does not look good?"

"Of course it looks good," he backpedaled. "But who's going to see you? You should save all that fancy stuff for when we got out on the town."

"*You* will see me," she answered with a sly smile. "That is only man for which I dress up."

If the clock wasn't ticking on the investigation into old man Geist's disappearance, he might've thrown her down on the bed right then and there. But the clock *was* ticking.

"You look *spectacular*," he said, emphasizing the superlative. "Are you ready?"

"Always." The smile broadened.

"That'll have to wait. Come on – let's go see a man about a murder. Maybe."

For just an instant the pout returned, but it was quickly replaced by the expectant look that had endeared her to Derek in the first place. No matter what was happening, she was game. The PI made sure he had his knife, a can of pepper spray disguised as a pump suntan lotion dispenser, and a stun-gun sheathed in a cellphone case. He felt a bit naked without his favorite 9mm, but figured he could always explain away the low tech accoutrements as personal protection. Cops'd probably just confiscate them. The pistol, however... might land him in jail. He only hoped whoever was behind Geist's disappearance was more the *man overboard* type than the *bullet between the eyes* type.

CHAPTER 6

There was still a line of Toyota van cabs waiting at the foot of the gangway as Derek and Olga emerged from the Princess. And Ms. Lansky, the Purser, was still facilitating the departure of passengers when the PI approached her.

"Hey, can you do me a favor?" he asked without introduction.

"Of course, Mr. DiLaurain! Just name it."

"Do you happen to know a cabbie we can hire by the day? Someone who won't rip us off and will be there when we tell him to be?"

"I think we can find you someone," she said, pulling out her cellphone and scanning the Contacts. She punched a number and waited. "Remmy – Miss Lansky from the Fantasy Princess," she began when the call was answered. "I'm fine, thank you. Hey, I have a passenger here who is doing some work for us, and he needs a cab on-call for a day or two. Are you available?" She listened to the response. "Good! How much – for the day?" She listened some more, until something she heard made her scrunch up her face as if she'd taken a bite out of a bitter lemon. "Remmy – I thought we had a good professional relationship!" she chided. "Save those prices for the tourists." Derek could see why she held the position she did.

Ms. Lansky listened some more. "Better, but I think $50 a day less would secure the job," she wheedled. Remmy the cab driver apparently thought better of his gouging and capitulated. She filled him in on the bare outlines of the job before hanging up. "He'll be here in ten minutes," she told Derek as she replaced the phone in her jacket pocket.

"We can trust him?"

"Once he makes a deal, he'll stick to it. It's getting him to see reality that's sometimes difficult."

"Don't you know anyone who'd be a bit more grateful for the job?"

She chuckled. "In Bermuda? People here would rather not work than work for less than they think they should get."

"And that's oftentimes more than it's worth?"

"Almost always. It's a national epidemic. If they don't watch out, they'll kill the golden goose. There's too much competition these days to take a 'my way or the highway' attitude."

"Well, as long as this Remmy is there when we need him."

"He will be."

Exactly ten minutes later a bright blue van pulled up right at the end of the gangway.

"That's him," the Purser announced, waving to the driver as he climbed out of the taxi. Derek took one look and almost asked for another cab.

The cabby was wearing bright pink knee-length shorts (in the Bermuda tradition), a 'Save the Planet' t-shirt, sported a long graying beard that looked as if it hadn't been trimmed since Harrison Ford appeared in the first *Star Wars* flick, and was wearing some kind of a sock/turban over his hair.

"Are you sure?" Derek asked the Purser.

"Don't be put off by his looks. He's a good driver."

"If you say so."

As they walked down the gangway, Olga bent low and whispered to Derek: "He look like drugs man."

"Yeh," was all the PI could answer.

But by the time they made it to the end of the steel ramp, the PI had pulled himself together and was ready to meet his new 'associate'.

"You must be Remmy," he said, reaching up for a handshake.

"I am, and you are DiLaurain?" the cabby answered with a warm smile and firm shake.

"*Mister* DiLaurain, or Derek," he said. "And this is my girlfriend – Olga."

The warm smile became even broader. "Bermuda-ful!" he said with such enthusiasm that Olga took a half-step back in spite of herself. She shook his hand demurely, trying to ignore his laser-like stare.

"Cute," Derek groused. "But we're in a bit of a hurry. Can we get a move on?"

"Sure thing, Boss," the cabby said. "Hop in."

Remmy opened a rear door for Olga and helped her into the van. Derek didn't wait for assistance, heading straight to the front passenger door – only he'd forgotten (if he'd ever known) that the Bermudians drive on the left side of the road. He found himself facing the steering wheel.

"Sorry Boss, no can do," Remmy said, assuming Derek intended to drive himself. "No foreign driver's licenses recognized here on the Island."

"Yeh, sure, that's cool," the PI fumbled to cover his mistake. "It's all yours."

He quickly shuffled around to the opposite side of the van and opened the door. There on the passenger seat, as if it had just materialized out of thin air, Derek found a stack of foam seat cushions positioned to lift him up to dashboard-level. It took him a few moments to climb atop the eight or nine inch mountain of foam, but when he did he managed to secure his seatbelt without difficulty.

"Ms. Lansky mentioned that you might appreciate a higher seat," Remmy said as he fired up the Toyota.

"Yeh, it's good. Thanks." He hated to admit it, but he was impressed. Usually he spent the entire ride in a cab staring at the back of the seat in front of him or directly into an air-conditioning vent. Bermuda was supposed to have sights worth seeing, so this arrangement would work well. If, that is, his hearing didn't give out first. As the engine roared to life, so did the radio, playing Bob Marley's *Redemption* at volumes that vibrated the fillings in his teeth.

Remmy said something to him, but all he heard was a muffled mumble, totally eclipsed by the Wailers' bassline.

"Hey, I like Marley as well as the next guy," Derek objected, trying to maintain some semblance of goodwill with the cabby while shouting at the top of his lungs to be heard, "but do you think you could turn it down a little?! If I'd wanted to go to Jamaica, I would've gone to Jamaica."

"No problem, Boss. Where to?"

"You don't need to call me that – *Boss*."

"Just a habit, B... Mr. D. Where we headed?"

Derek could see it'd be a constant battle to convince the driver to call him by his first name, so decided to just go with the flow. "Let's try the Coral Queen." He turned to Olga. "We'll talk to Arnie first."

"The Coral Queen!" Remmy remarked with inflection that suggested he was impressed with their destination. "You two must be richer than you look. Most cruise passengers stay onboard overnight while the ship's in port."

Derek considered taking offense, but decided it wasn't worth his time. "Actually, we're going there to interview someone."

"What are you – some kind of writer, or something?"

"No, nothing like that."

"TV reporter? Radio?"

"Nope." Derek knew better than to let slip any information about an ongoing investigation. Particularly on a little island like Bermuda, half the population would know about it before the day was over.

Remmy waited, as if hoping Derek would expand on his monosyllabic response. When no additional info was forthcoming, he settled back into his seat and drove. As they pulled away from the relatively touristy Dockside environs, Derek was increasingly happy ol' Remmy had brought along the stack of cushions – the views were fantastic! Only a few minutes from the relatively industrial feel of the outskirts to the docks, the van crossed a miniature bridge that led to a tiny village of multi-colored homes dotting the landscape. Pale greens and blues and pinks competed with the dazzling blue-green of the ocean. Brilliant white roofs topped each and every one of the modest structures, each a marvel of multi-terraced levels.

"What's with the white roofs?" the PI asked. "To reflect the sun?"

"Actually, our roofs are made of limestone, coated with a thin wash of cement," Remmy began with the practiced ease of someone who's repeated the same description innumerable times before. "They have those steps to channel rainwater to cisterns underneath the houses – we have no supply of fresh water on the Island."

"*No* fresh water?"

"Not naturally."

"Houses are small," Olga spoke up. "I thought they are bigger – for movie star."

The driver laughed. "Oh, you'll see more than a few of those all over the Island. But most folk live a whole lot more modestly."

"Like who?" Olga asked, her interest piqued. "What movie star?"

"Oh, Michael Douglas for one. He's from here, you know." The sense of pride in his voice was unmistakable.

"Michael Douglas is a Bermudian?!" Derek asked.

"His momma was from the Island."

"Who else?" Olga prodded.

"Well, there's the former mayor of New York – Bloomberg, and the Italian politician Berlusconi, and a bunch of rich folk you and I never heard of."

"No movie star?"

"Oh we get our share. John Wayne, Nick Nolte, Brooke Shields, even John Lennon lived here for a while. And of course the Royal Family comes down from time to time."

"Who are those people?" Olga asked Derek softly.

"Except for the Queen and her people, the rest were all famous actors, and a singer – most of 'em dead now, I think."

"No Konstantin Khabensky, Aleksei Chadov, or Aleksandra Tabakova?"

Remmy looked to Derek with confusion in his eyes. "Haven't never heard of them. I could axe around…"

"Axe?" Derek said before he could edit himself.

"You know, axe questions. See if anyone's heard of 'em."

"Ah, yes. No, I don't think you need to *axe* anyone. She was just curious. Weren't you, honey buns?"

"I want to see movie star," the Russian beauty said with a hint of petulance.

"We'll see what's playing at the local theater – *after* we find out what's happened to Mr. Geist. How's that sound?"

She grunted with disdain, and they drove on in silence.

They drove through quaint, if often less than spectacular surroundings for fifteen minutes or so, until the cab veered off to the right on South Road just a short distance from an extremely picturesque lighthouse. Minutes later they were staring at spectacular jagged rock flows extending out into the bluest blue-green water Derek had ever seen.

"Wow. Pretty nice, huh?" the PI asked his travel mate.

"You never see Crimea," she said with ill-concealed disdain.

"True enough. But this'll do until I get there." There was a brief moment of silence as the car wound its way along the stunning southern coastline. "That's where your people stole the whole island back from the Ukraine, right?" he added without thinking.

"Crimea is peninsula."

"Yeh, well until they stop shooting each other I think I'll stick to Bermuda."

"That'd be my choice," Remmy spoke up.

"Crimea always Russian. Khrushchev was idiot," Olga mumbled.

"Yeh, well their current top dog isn't much better."

"Putin not dog," she challenged.

"Just a figure of speech, honey. Just a figure of speech."

When the cab finally pulled off the main road and passed through a gated entrance worthy of Beverly Hills, the PI knew they'd arrived.

"Here you go," Remmy said as they pulled up in front of a huge pillared portico that would've made President Obama feel right at home. "The Coral Queen."

For the first time, Olga was impressed. "Ochen Khorosho. Wonder if have caviar," she muttered to herself as the driver held the door for her.

"Okay, look," Derek explained to her as they walked into the cavernous reception area, "I've got to talk to the missing guy's son. Do you want to come along, or would you rather hang out at the pool – or the bar?"

She thought briefly. "Pool. Come back soon."

"My preference, exactly." He led Olga over to the Concierge. "Think you can find a good spot by the pool for my girl while I take care of some business here?" he asked, offering the man a folded ten dollar bill.

The hotel employee looked up at Olga, then down at Derek, before casually accepting the ten.

"It would be my pleasure, sir," he said – his eyes, backed by a winning smile, once again on Olga.

"Good. Make sure she's comfortable. I'll settle the bill when I swing by to pick her up."

With the girlfriend taken care of, the PI waddled over to the reception area. A conversation between two older guests stopped in mid-sentence as they both turned to watch the little man approach.

"Good morning, folks!" Derek greeted them cheerfully.

The woman's eyes flew open as if she'd just sat on a whoopee cushion.

"Morning," the man said even as he grabbed his wife by the arm and led her quickly away.

"Don't get out much I suppose," he said to the attractive young woman behind the reception desk.

"I suppose," she said with an amused smile. "May I help you, sir?"

"Arnold Geist Junior? I believe he's staying here. Would you please ring him up and tell him Derek DiLaurain is here to see him – tell him it's about his father."

"Is Mr. Geist expecting you?"

"Probably. Or someone like me."

The woman's eyebrows arched, but she picked up the phone. After a brief conversation she turned back to Derek.

"Mr. Geist will see you. He's in the Royals Suite. Do you know how to get there?"

"Marry a Royal?" he joked. To the blank stare that greeted his quip he replied, "I don't, no."

The receptionist tapped a bell on the counter and a middle-aged bellboy appeared from the ether.

"Please show Mr. DiLaurain to the Royals Suite," she requested.

"My pleasure," the man said with so little enthusiasm that Derek very much doubted the sentiment.

He thanked the young woman and turned to follow the bellboy.

"Do you have luggage, sir?" the bellboy asked, glancing around as if he believed that Derek had hidden his bags behind a planter somewhere.

"I'm not staying," the PI answered. "Not up to my standards."

The bellboy looked as if he'd been hit between the eyes with a 2 x 4, but said nothing as he led the way.

Wandering through the Coral Queen was akin to watching a segment of *Lifestyles of the Rich and Famous* in 3D – every aspect of the hotel had been handled beautifully. From the polished dark wood that graced walls, doors, and window sills, to the lush carpeting underfoot (not the multi-colored indoor/outdoor stuff you see at Motel 8), fine paintings on the walls (not faded prints of schlock), to the chandeliers, cut glass vases and eye-popping fresh flowers, the Queen was exactly as its name would suggest.

By the time the bellboy rang the doorbell at the Royals Suite, it was clear to the PI that Arnold Jr. was not a man to skimp on his vacation digs. He waited patiently with the sullen hotel employee for someone to answer the door, a wait that stretched on interminably.

"What, did the guy forget we were coming in the three minutes it took for us to get here?" he mumbled aloud.

The bellboy sighed but kept silent.

Finally, more than two minutes later, the door opened to reveal Arnold Geist Jr. himself, resplendent in a loud Hawaiian print shirt, carrying a cellphone in his left hand.

"I'm very sorry," he mouthed, all the while keeping the mouthpiece of the phone pressed against his chest while motioning for them to come in. "Had to take this. Have a seat."

Derek began to do as he was told, forgetting all about the bellboy until the Bermudian cleared his throat loudly.

"Oh yeh, right," the PI said, digging into his pocket. "Do you take American money?"

"No problem."

He peeled off a one dollar bill and handed it to the man. "Thanks."

The man looked as if someone had farted surreptitiously, but took the money and left without comment. Derek was not so reserved.

"What? You think it's worth more than a buck to walk me to this room?!" he shouted after the now quick-stepping bellboy. "You're lucky you got *that*!"

He suddenly realized where he was and peeked into the suite to see if Arnie had noticed his outburst, but the eldest Geist was out on the patio chatting away with animated hand movements and shouts of his own. Derek closed the door behind him as he moved closer to see what he could hear through the closed sliding glass door.

"I don't give a damn how many shares he owned!" the elder Geist was shouting. "If he's gone, then my mother has voting rights... Don't worry – I can handle her."

Derek had sidled up so close to the door that his head was almost touching the glass, when a door that led off the main room opened with a well-oiled whoosh and the same attractive trophy wife he'd noticed the previous night onboard the Princess emerged without any advance warning. She was obviously as surprised to see him as he was to see her, for her mouth opened in a wide 'O' as if she thought for an instant about screaming. She didn't appear quite the trophy as the night before, wearing no makeup and with her freshly-washed hair sticking out in every conceivable direction. She quickly pulled her thick white terrycloth robe tight around her, but not before the PI caught a glimpse of a tasty set of knockers (or *beautifully proportioned breasts*, as Derek mused the Geist crew might describe them.)

"Oh! You frightened me," she said awkwardly.

"Yeh, big guys like me often have that effect on people," Derek said without a hint of a smile.

"Oh, no, it's just, I didn't know Arnie had a guest," she fumbled before getting her feet under her and stepping out into the living room.

"Name's Derek DiLaurain. I'm a private investigator," he introduced himself, pulling out a card to hand to her.

"Oh, yes, of course. You're here about poor Arnold, aren't you?"

"Actually, I'm here about *rich* Arnold. Unless you know something I don't," he said.

"What? Oh, no, I don't *know* anything. But he's been gone so long now, I just assumed…"

"We try not to assume anything – Mrs. Geist, is it?"

"Yes. Brenda. My name's Brenda." He could see her pull herself together right before his eyes. "May I offer you something?"

"Glass of water?"

"We have juice."

"No thanks – just a glass of water would be great."

She padded off to the kitchen. "So *is* there any more news about Arnold's father?" she asked back over her shoulder.

"Nothing firm. The police *have* found a hat that belonged to Mr. Geist."

"Oh my goodness!" the woman shouted. "That's bad, isn't it? Do they think he fell overboard?"

"It'd be pretty hard – falling overboard in a wheelchair. From what little I know of the ship, there's no place a passenger would normally go where a wheelchair could accidentally roll over the edge."

Brenda Geist came back into the living room carrying the glass of water. "So what are you saying? Do they think someone *pushed* Arnold off the ship?" Her eyes were wide.

"Too early to even know if Mr. Geist went overboard. At this point all they have is the hat."

Once again Derek watched the woman collect herself. "Well thank goodness for that," she said as she handed him the glass. "We've had enough bad news lately."

"Oh?" Derek came back, his PI antennae on full alert. "What kind of news was that?"

Arnie's wife glanced around quickly, as if double-checking that her husband was still out on the balcony. "Well, there may be a problem with the books – at the company," she said, her voice barely more than a whisper. "There may be some money missing."

"How much money?" the PI asked nonchalantly.

Brenda peeked back at Arnie again. "Two hundred million dollars."

Derek whistled. "That's more than *some* money, at least in my checking account. What happened?"

"I really shouldn't be telling you all this," she started, clearly nervous, "but…"

Before she could finish, the sliding glass door to the balcony slid open and her husband came back into the suite.

"Sorry," he said, dropping his cellphone into his pants pocket. "I had to take that call. Ah, I see you've met my wife."

"I have. We were just chatting."

"Is that water? Can I get you anything stronger? A scotch perhaps?" He headed straight for the glass and chrome wet bar.

"A little early for me." It wasn't, really, but he didn't want the brothers to pigeonhole him as the prototypical drunken PI.

"Brenda?" he asked as he poured himself a stiff one.

"No, thank you dear."

"Normally I'd agree with you, but today has been a particularly trying day."

"Already?" Derek asked.

"Yeh. Already." Arnie shut the bar and came over to sit directly opposite the sofa where Derek had positioned himself.

"So, I understand you're looking into my father's disappearance. Do you have news?"

"They found Dad's hat!" Brenda offered breathlessly.

"They have? Who has? Tell me," he directed his questions to the PI.

"A person at the beach found it and turned it over to the Bermuda police."

"So? What are they thinking?" He didn't seem particularly upset by the news.

"Nothing concrete. At this point it's just a hat."

"But it could suggest…" He paused, leaving the conclusion unspoken.

"It could suggest a lot of things," Derek finished the sentence for him. "But until they have more information, it's all just speculation."

"So that's why you're here – to get more information?"

"That's about the size of it. Have you got a few minutes?"

"Of course! Whatever insights I can provide."

He decided to hit the eldest son right between the eyes. "Good. So, what's this I hear about your company missing a good chuck of cash?"

Arnie glanced over at his wife, who feigned interest in the leaves of a nearby plant. He tried to keep a straight face, but his eyes flamed.

"Where'd you hear that?" he said with admirable self-control.

"Around. It seems it's common knowledge among the big-buck set back in New York."

"What?!" His face paled.

"That's what I'm hearing."

"It can't be," he mumbled to himself, shaking his head slowly. It took a few seconds before he remembered that Derek was still sitting there. "I…"

The PI decided to give him a little push. "Two hundred million? Is that about right?"

Arnie blinked twice as though in shock. "Yes, yes that's about right."

"Any ideas yet where it went?"

The veil fell from Arnie's eyes. "I don't see how this has any bearing on Dad's disappearance," he said with the kind of assuredness Derek would expect from a big-time CEO.

"Two hundred million dollars disappears from your company, your father disappears a few days later, and you don't see the relevance?" The PI stared at his quarry, challenging him to find fault with the logic. He couldn't.

"Ah. I see. Looking at it that way, I can see how you'd come to that conclusion."

"What other way *can* I look at it?"

Arnie looked away; Derek usually took that to mean the person was lying to him. "Well, we haven't had time to do a thorough audit of our books…"

"You must have some ideas."

"Of course, but at this point it's all pure speculation."

"Understood. What are some of the possibilities under consideration?"

The eldest son took a long sip of his scotch, then paused for a painfully long moment. Derek could almost hear the wheels whirring.

"Well, of course it could simply be a clerical error," he began.

"A TWO HUNDRED MILLION DOLLAR CLERICAL ERROR?!" Derek responded with a bit more emphasis than he'd intended. "Who's your CFO? Donald Duck?"

"Actually, it's my brother, Aaron," he said, his voice suggesting more than just the fact. Or at least that's how Derek heard it.

"*Aaron* is your CFO? The wild man who gambles millions and dates starlets? Are you guys nuts?"

"He has an MBA from the University of Chicago," Arnie responded defensively. "He's a very smart guy."

"And he has a screw loose! Is he the prime suspect then?"

"No! Of course not!" Arnie replied. "It just happens, he's the CFO."

"Did he discover the shortage?"

Arnie fidgeted with his glass. "Aaron was traveling last week."

"Vegas?"

"Macau," his older brother said softly. He looked up at Derek as if daring him to verbalize the obvious.

"Okay. So it could be a clerical error," Derek said instead, deciding to keep the older brother talking as long as possible. "What else?"

"Well, there are a number of people in the organization who have access to large sums of money."

"Including your father?"

Once again, the CEO paused. "Yeh, Dad had that kind of access." Absolutely non-committal.

"And Aaron."

"Obviously." A note of irritation.

"And you?"

His features hardened. "Look, Mr. DiLaurain…" He pronounced each syllable as if it were sticking in his throat. "What are you suggesting? That my brother, or *I* might be responsible for my father's disappearance?"

"Just asking questions," Derek said calmly. "Not drawing any conclusions yet."

"I'm not sure I like the tone of your *questions*."

Derek had seen the type before: big, powerful businessman, used to everyone kissing his butt and doing what he wanted. Not used to explaining himself to anyone, let alone some shrimpy little private investigator.

"It's either me or the local cops," Derek explained. "*Someone* has to answer these questions, and I thought you might prefer talking to me."

He could see the thunderclouds gathering on Arnie's brow, but as quickly as they'd appeared, with a deep sigh they were gone. "Okay. I understand. 'Just doing your duty', and all that. So, yes, I did – do – have access to the company funds. I'm the CEO, for Chrissakes. If *anyone* has access, it'd be me."

"But you don't have any idea what happened to the $200 million?" He held up his hands. "Just asking."

The CEO was back under control. "No, I don't have any idea what happened to the money. But we've got the accountants hard at work. They'll track it down before too long."

"When did you find out – that the money was missing?"

"A day or two before we came onboard the Princess. Great way to start a vacation…"

"Not the best, huh? How did everyone react? I mean, your father, your brothers…"

"How do you *think* they reacted? They weren't dancing in the aisles, if that's what you mean."

"Did they yell, curse, throw something?"

At that, the eldest Geist brother paused, trying to remember. "Dad was a little hot. I think he swore. Aaron, not so much. Just shook his head."

"And Ayden?"

"Ayden never reacts to anything." The way he said it left the impression he wasn't enamored with his brother's self-control.

"That's not fair," his wife spoke for the first time since he'd come back in. "Ayden is quiet, but he's not comatose. He just doesn't fly off the handle at every little thing." This time it seemed to the PI that it was Arnie in the crosshairs.

"Like me? Is that what you're getting at?" Arnie said crossly.

"I didn't say that," Brenda answered, but her tone suggested the exact opposite.

"Yeh, well sometimes you have to take into account the environment a person lives in, what he has to put up with."

Brenda was about to fire back, when Derek spoke up.

"Hate to interrupt a family discussion, but can we get back to your father, and the missing money?"

Arnie glared at his wife, who grunted and got up to go back into the adjoining bedroom.

"Yeh, yeh sure," Arnie said after following his wife's departure with a poisonous glare. "What else do you need to know?"

"Well, was there any reason why your father would *want* to disappear? I mean, have you noticed anything unusual about his behavior in the last few weeks, or months?"

"I don't know," Arnie muttered, "he's old. Old people are strange. They say things, do things…"

"What kind of things?"

"I don't know, all sorts. I mean, in the last little bit Dad was talking about selling his shares in the company and retiring – really retiring. But I don't know if anyone took him seriously."

"So he hasn't been fully retired these last twenty years or so?"

Arnie's lips curled. "You could say that."

"Has he kept a hand-in at the company?"

"And a foot, and a leg, and every other damn part of his anatomy. I was kind of hoping he was going to announce his *second* retirement on this cruise."

"But no such luck, huh?"

"Nah. Not a word."

"How about the will – was anyone upset about who got what?"

Arnie leaned back and took a deep sip of his whiskey. "Maybe. Probably. Except for Aaron, nobody else said anything, at least not to me."

"Nothing from Ayden?"

"Like I said…"

"How about you? I understand that you didn't react all that well to the announcement."

He shrugged. "I suppose you could say that. I've done the majority of the heavy lifting at the company for the past twenty plus years, increased our net worth by something like 65 per cent, and I get the same share as my brothers? Hell, the same as his nurse?! I mean, it doesn't really matter…"

"How's that?"

"Well, I get a pretty good package from the company as-is, and it's not like we're hurting for anything. And when Mother dies, I assume we'll all get a bigger chunk. But that's not the point. The old man should've recognized my contribution."

Derek had to restrain himself from shaking his head and commenting. He'd seen it a million times before: a wealthy, successful, powerful person brought to their emotional knees by some perceived slight by one or both parents. He was always amazed at the grip family dynamics had on people. The long arm of genetics never really let go.

Instead, he kept his poker face and continued. "And Aaron? What was his beef?"

"Eh, about the same I guess. Best ask him."

"I'll do that. But how do you see it? Did he expect a bigger slice too?"

"Aaron always expects a bigger slice," Arnie muttered. "But he never wants to work for it."

"Word has it he's a bit of a playboy."

"Ha!" his older brother sneered. "He's a bit of a loose cannon who likes to gamble – is that what you'd call a 'playboy'?"

"Not so much the ladies' man?"

Arnie looked as if he was going to snarl, but caught himself. "No, not so much a *ladies'* man."

The way he pronounced *ladies* made the PI take notice, but he decided not to press it. Instead he made a note to ask Brady to look into the younger brother's sexual proclivities. For the time being, he felt as if he'd gotten a pretty good overview of the oldest brother, and his wife, and it was time to get down to specifics.

"All right. Now I know that this next series of questions will probably rub you the wrong way, but you've gotta understand that they have to be asked. By me now, and probably by the local cops in a short while."

Arnie took a long sip of whiskey, shaking his head in disgust. "If this turns out to be the Old Man's idea of a joke, I may throw him overboard myself." He turned back to Derek. "Go ahead."

"Last night, after you and Aaron stormed out of the family get-together…"

"I wouldn't say we 'stormed out'," Arnold Jr. interrupted.

"Okay. Then after you and your brother left the dining room *rather abruptly*, where did you go?"

The disgusted look on Junior's face turned to a scowl. "Jesus Christ! So you think *we* might have had something to do with Dad's disappearance?"

"Your father is missing, and nobody knows where or how," Derek explained patiently. "Until we do, *everyone* is a suspect."

"Okay, fine," Arnie said, but in a tone that strongly suggested that everything was *not* fine. "Aaron and I went out to the deck for a smoke, and to let off some steam."

"What did you talk about?"

"That's personal!" Arnie barked.

"Nothing's personal in a missing persons case. I can assure you the police will ask the same question. Isn't it better to have a chance to rehearse – or maybe I should say remember, before you talk to them?"

"You're a real piece of work, you know that?" Arnie asked, staring at the PI with absolutely no hint of affection.

"So I've been told. You gonna tell me, or will I have to get it from the cops?"

Exasperation dripped from every syllable. "We talked about what an asshole our father is, and whether he was poking that nurse of his – to give her $25 million, I mean. TWENTY-FIVE MILLION!"

For the first time, Arnie showed real emotion.

"That's not so much for a man with your father's resources," Derek tweaked.

"Not so much for Dad, maybe. But it's too damn much for that Latina bimbo! I mean, she's already making good money, she gets to travel all over the world, stay in the best hotels, go on cruises… What the hell."

"Was Aaron as *displeased* as you seem to be?"

"*Displeased*?! If you think I'm displeased, then Aaron was downright pissed! From his vantage point, every penny that goes to her is one less he can put on red or black in… Macau, or wherever."

"How about you? Surely it doesn't make that big a difference to someone who makes $8 million a year."

The eldest son twitched ever so slightly.

"Who told you that?"

"Got it on the Internet," Derek said with a grin. "You'd be amazed what you can find online."

"Don't believe everything you read."

"So you don't make $8 million a year?"

Arnie hesitated, as if weighing his words. "That includes stock options. It's not a cash figure," he eventually admitted.

"Still, not a drop in the bucket. Why were you so *displeased*?"

"I… I mean, it's a slap in our faces. Twenty-five million for *her*? For what? I don't care how good her massages are, or what she massages, for that matter. She's a nurse! We built the goddamn company. We've been with him through the good times and the bad. We've put up with all his crap…"

"Like what?" Derek interrupted.

"What?" Arnie asked, suddenly thrown off-course.

"You said you've put up with all his crap – like what?"

The CEO made a face. "We don't wash our laundry in public."

"If something has happened to your father, the police are gonna ask you the same question, and your answers will become a part of the court record."

"Great," he muttered, taking another swig of whiskey. "That's all we need."

"Is it really so bad? What'd he do, beat the kids? Cheat on the wife?" The PI was being flip, and so was caught off guard when Arnie's eyes opened wide.

"Did you get *that* from the Internet too?" he growled.

"Just a hunch."

Arnie looked out at the blue-green water just a stone's throw from the back of his suite. "You know, everyone thinks that wealthy people are somehow better, or at least more sophisticated than the average slob in the streets," he began, his voice low. "If they only knew." His chuckle was humorless. "Guys who make it, who *really* make it, put everything into their business. All their money, all their energy, all their everything. Doesn't leave much for anything – or any*body* – else. You know what I mean?"

Derek nodded, unwilling to break his train of thought.

"Dad was like that. It was the business, every day, every hour of the day. I can't tell you how many ballgames, or recitals, or... just about anything he promised to attend and then didn't. Oh, he was always apologetic, or usually anyhow. But I doubt we saw him much more than a few hours a week during my entire childhood. We kids joke that we all joined the business because it was the only way to spend time with him."

"Must've been hard on your mother."

He shrugged. "I guess. I mean, he made enough time to father the three of us, so at least she saw him every now and then. And she had her own life: the Club, on the Board at our school, whatever. At least we saw her."

"And the beatings?"

"He didn't really *beat* us." Something about the way he said it made Derek doubt him.

"But he did hit you."

"He... believed in corporal punishment. Just like his father had."

"How often?"

"Not so often. He wasn't around enough to make it a regular occurrence."

"And you probably got the worst of it, being the oldest."

"Until we were teenagers, yeh. Ayden was always the quiet, studious kid. And Aaron was always the youngest, Dad's little pet. Until he hit 13 or so. Then, he came into his own. Girls, gambling, pot – you name it, Aaron tried it."

"How'd your father react?"

"How do you think? First he tried to beat it out of him, then he tried cutting his allowance, then he sent him off to boarding school."

"Military?"

"Same thing. Extreme regimentation. A ton of rules."

"Did it work?"

"Do you mean did it make Aaron a better *citizen*? A better Geist? No way. Just the opposite, actually. It made him less obvious. Sneakier."

Derek sat and waited. One thing he'd learned from Brady: when you're interviewing someone who seems to want to tell you something, give him enough time to make the decision. Most of the time, he'll decide to talk. The silence in the room was more powerful than any question, any accusation. Five seconds. Ten. He was about to ask another question, when Arnie began to talk of his own accord.

"You know," he said softly, "I'm not even sure how I'd feel if something *has* happened to the Old Man. It's not as though we're close, or have ever been for that matter. And he certainly doesn't do much at the business, other than screw things up every now and then, just for the hell of it. It's almost like he's a ghost, an apparition that appears whenever *it* feels like it."

"How about the others – your brothers? Your mother?"

"I don't know. You'll have to ask them. But I don't see how they could feel much differently than I do. I mean, it's not like he's an actual member of the family. Not in any real sense."

Derek could hear in his voice a weariness, a sadness. And he knew that the interview was over. But he tried a couple of last questions, on the off-chance that he'd strike a nerve.

"Anybody outside the inner circle have a problem with your father?"

Arnie laughed dismissively. "Half the builders and real estate investors in the country. But anyone in particular? Not that I know of."

Derek nodded as he jotted a note. "You said a while ago that you hoped this wasn't your father's idea of a joke. What did you mean?"

Arnie stared off into space. At first the PI thought he wasn't going to answer. But then, haltingly, he did. "My father has always wanted to be the center of the universe. Not just *our* universe, the *entire* universe. And now that he's getting older, it's even worse. It's as if he can't stand to think that someone else is running his precious company, and getting credit for it."

"Does he dislike it enough to pull a stunt like disappearing at sea?"

He shrugged. "Don't know. I don't really know the man well enough to say one way or the other. But it wouldn't surprise me, that I *can* say."

The interview concluded, Derek swung by the resort pool to pick up his girlfriend, and found her chatting amiably with the bartender at the swim-up infinity pool.

"Quite the pool," he called out as he approached from behind the barkeep. Upon hearing his voice, the twenty-something employee turned and reacted with the surprise Derek had grown accustomed to.

"Need a drink?" the bartender asked without a great deal of warmth.

"Nope." The tiny PI stood there, smiling at Olga. "Quite the babe, too," he went on, ignoring the staring pool man.

"Are you a guest?" the bartender asked, obviously irritated to have his *intimate* conversation interrupted.

"Nope."

"Well, I'm afraid this is a *private* pool," the young man enunciated with enough venom to shake the average non-guest. Derek's smile widened.

"What's a beautiful babe like you doing in a dump like this?" he asked Olga, who batted her eyelashes starlet-style.

"Waiting for right man," she said seductively.

"I said, this is a *private* pool," the bartender interrupted, his anger growing.

"Well, here I am," Derek went on with his little play-acting, ignoring the young guy completely. "Why don't we blow this overgrown bathtub?"

"Sir!" the bartender insisted, but Derek was having no part of it. He reached out his hand and helped Olga to her feet.

"I've got something I wanna show you," he teased.

"Oh? What is that?" Olga played along.

"It's long, and hard, and …HOT!"

"Oooo. You will show me?"

"I'll do more than that, Sweetheart. Much more than that."

As they walked away, Derek glanced back at the stunned, red-faced bartender and winked.

CHAPTER 7

The cab ride from the Coral Queen to the
Hibiscus didn't take more than ten minutes.

Remmy asked about the meeting, but Derek
deflected the question with some non sequitur that the
cabbie accepted without comment. They'd driven the
rest of the way, along a coastline of jagged volcanic
rocks jutting out into the brilliant turquoise sea, in
complete silence, except for the steel-drum rhythms of
reggae playing – softly – on the car radio.

The entrance to the Hibiscus wasn't nearly as
grandiose as that to the Coral Queen, but still spoke of
wealth and privilege. The hedges were impeccably
trimmed, flower beds exploded with color every few
yards, and the reception area was decorated with the
kind of low-key but expensive tchotchke that you'd
expect to see in an elegant boutique or gallery. Not at all
the kind of joint Derek would expect to find the
youngest Geist son.

"Derek DiLaurain, for Mr. Aaron Geist," he
announced to the elegantly coiffed desk clerk. To his

relief, the woman hadn't blinked an eye when he
waddled into the reception area. Perhaps that was what
defined a truly upscale establishment – the ability to
accept whatever came through its doors as if they'd seen
it a thousand times before.

The woman glanced at her elegant, ultra-thin
computer screen, and ran her elegant, highly polished
nails down a list of guests.

"I'm afraid we do not have anyone by that name,"
she announced with something less than total concern.

"Well, he's here. He checked in this morning,
probably around 10 a.m."

The woman feigned looking at the list once again.

"I'm afraid there's no one by that name…" she
began.

"This is police business," Derek interrupted. "If
you don't want your *hotel* swarming with uniformed
cops, I suggest you call whoever checked in around 10,
and tell them I'm here." He stared at her as if daring a
reply. The woman blinked once and picked up the
phone. She turned away from Derek and spoke quietly
into the receiver. She nodded unconsciously at the reply.

"Mr. *Aaron* is in bungalow C, around the pool to
the left, overlooking the sea," she said as she hung up
the phone.

"You're *too* kind," Derek replied, with the kind of F-you intonation that had gotten him into innumerable scrapes, but which gave him immeasurable satisfaction.

The PI reconnected with his girlfriend as she emerged from the Ladies room and they wound their way through the hallways and park-like grounds, finally circling the Olympic size pool and arriving at a line of white limestone-roofed *cottages* that reflected the subtle elegance of the Hibiscus. Olga once again elected to remain poolside, while Derek quickly checked out the immediate surroundings, looking for alternate egress if necessary. Waves splashed playfully against the cliffs just twenty feet or so from the front (back?) door to bungalow C. He knocked. No reply. So he knocked again. He heard a glass door slide open and footsteps flap on ceramic tile.

The door swung open to reveal Aaron Geist, a drink cradled lovingly in his hand, wearing a tropical print bathing suit and sandals – the kind that look like cheap junk but probably cost a hundred bucks. He stared down at the PI through silvery sunglasses, the reflective lenses giving Derek a Geist-eye view of himself.

"Yeh?" he asked after a few seconds.

"My name is…" the PI began, but Aaron cut him off.

"I know your name. What I want to know is why the hell are you here bothering me?"

There are two ways to deal with a jerk like Geist: 1) punch him straight in the balls and step over his writhing body, or 2) smile disarmingly and hope the guy is so taken aback he doesn't do #1 to you. Derek chose #2.

"I thought we might talk a bit," he said with such sincerity that even *he* would've given him a minute or two of his time if their roles were reversed. "About your father."

Aaron stared, less than convinced. "What about the old bastard?"

"May I come in?"

"Will this take long? I've got a massage coming in..." he glanced at his Patek Phillipe watch, "fifteen minutes."

"That might be enough."

"It'll have to be," he announced as he turned and walked back through the cottage and out the sliding glass doors to where an extremely attractive, extremely young woman in a nearly nonexistent bikini lay stretched out on a sunning bed, an umbrella'ed drink sitting by her right hand.

"Edie, I need to talk to this little guy for a few minutes," he said to her perfectly tanned back. "Why don't you go use the ladies room?"

"Oh? Oh…" the woman said as she turned over, one hand holding her bikini top in place while the other fished for her drink.

She got up without another word and left, all the while staring at Derek as if he'd just beamed down from an alien spaceship.

"Okay, the clock is ticking," the youngest Geist son said as he flopped down on a be-toweled lounger.

"Nice digs," Derek said, glancing around at the private pool, wet bar, and elaborate gas grill area.

"Is this an interview for Better Homes and Gardens, or what?" Aaron snapped.

"Actually, I've been hired to help locate your father."

"By whom?" Aaron asked, leaning back in his lounger to better catch the sun's rays.

"By the cruise company, and your mother," he answered as he scooted up into a chair that faced the supine Geist.

"Did you try looking up his butt? That's where he usually is."

"Do I detect a note of *displeasure*?" Derek asked with his usual casual subtlety.

"Damn right," Aaron said. "A whole symphony."

"Why's that? If I understand correctly, your father just announced last night that he's leaving you twenty-five million dollars in his will. Most people would think that's rather generous."

"Most people don't have my bills."

"Oh? Mortgage payments? Dental bills?" Derek couldn't help sticking it to pompous asses like Aaron.

"Not really any of your business, short stuff." Geist patted his forehead with a fluffy towel. "Do you have anything relevant to ask, or can I get back to my sunbathing?"

Derek let a moment pass for dramatic emphasis. "Your brother says you enjoy placing a bet or two."

"Which one?! I bet it was that little kiss-ass Ayden."

"You'd lose that bet."

"Doesn't matter. How I spend my money is my business."

"Unless your father doesn't turn up in the next little bit. Then it'll be police business."

"But you're not a cop, are you?"

"No. But if I tell my friends in the local constabulary that you were particularly evasive, uncooperative, and even downright hostile, I can tell you you'll be spending a good chunk of your Bermuda holiday talking to guys who *are* cops. Is that what you want?" He'd had enough of playing games with the spoiled Geist brat.

"Let me guess: Napoleon complex?" Geist sneered.

"Getting-to-the-bottom-of-things complex," Derek answered without giving an inch.

"Jesus Christ. Just my luck to get a midget with an attitude. Okay, alright, we'll play it your way. So what did you want to know?"

The PI glared at him, but kept his voice and temper modulated. "When I dig into things, how big are the gambling debts I'm going to find?"

Aaron tilted his head and pressed his lips together as if it pained him to even consider the prospect. "Too big," he finally said.

"Millions?"

Geist nodded sullenly.

"Over ten million?"

He glanced up at the ceiling. "Yeh. You happy now?"

"What are you, some kind of addict?"

"I *enjoy* gambling, okay?"

"And I enjoy a beer every now and then, but I don't drink ten million of them at one time."

"The money doesn't matter," Aaron muttered.

"Oh? Really? Then why were you so angry about only getting twenty-five million in the will? Figure it'd only last you a couple of weeks?"

Aaron's stare came to rest on his overpriced sandals. "You wouldn't understand."

"Try me."

He sighed and took another sip of his drink. After a long pause Derek began to think he'd decided against opening-up. But then he started, his voice soft, shaky. "You have any idea what it's like being the youngest son in a family like ours?" he began, glancing up at Derek. "Do you?"

"Can't say that I do. Why don't you tell me."

Another long pause. "In *our* family it means that the oldest kid got all the attention from the Old Man, the middle kid got a pat on the head from time to time, while the youngest, the youngest got bupkis, nada, nothing. Oh, my mother always took my side, always stood up to the Old Man, but all that got me was the nickname Momma's Boy." He traced his lips unconsciously with one finger. "Do you realize that my father never came to a single one of my birthday parties until I was 13? And the only reason he came to that one was because a business meeting got unexpectedly canceled and he had nowhere else to go. Otherwise, I would've gotten a present from him and Mom that he'd never seen, with a card that my mother had signed for him."

"A lot of parents work long hours," Derek said, trying to disguise his irritation.

"It's not the hours."

"Well what is it then!?" the PI snapped.

"I'm his son!" Aaron said with surprising emphasis. "I'm not just some employee who's been with him for a few years. I'm his flesh and blood. You'd think there'd be some recognition of that, wouldn't you?"

"Twenty five million dollars isn't recognition enough?"

"No. It's not." The finality was striking.

"But you got the same amount as your two brothers, didn't you?"

Geist shook his head in disgust. "I told you, it isn't the money!"

"We seem to be going in circles here."

Aaron stared at the PI. "All I wanted was a thank you," he said quietly. "A thank you for thirty years building *his* company. Not *ours*; his."

Derek marveled how differently people saw themselves from how others saw them. "Your brother Arnold seems to think he deserved some kind of thanks as well."

"He does. All three of us do. Even Ayden. The money is fine, but just once I'd like him to tell us that he recognizes all we've done for Geist & Sons. Just once."

"I hate to repeat myself, but doesn't twenty five million say that pretty clearly?"

A flush burst into Aaron's cheeks. "Does it? Or does it simply put us in the same category as a glorified nanny? That's what she is, you know. She calls herself a nurse, but that's just so she can give Dad his pills. Most of the time she just feeds him, changes his diaper, and pushes him around in his wheelchair. Nothing different than a nanny does for a two year-old. Probably a lot less. The three of us – my brothers and me – we *built* the company, from a little residential rental business to one of the largest commercial real estate companies in the *world*! The world!" His eyes shone, whether with anger, pride, or some combination, Derek wasn't certain.

"So if he's gone – permanently – the three of you take over the company?"

"The Board would have to give its okay, but I'm pretty certain we'd get the nod, yes."

"And that would mean more money, more authority, more… recognition?"

A small smile creased Aaron's lips. "Ah, you're thinking it sounds like a pretty good motive for doing away with the Old Man, is that it?"

"People have done worse for less."

"Or better." The youngest brother swept the air clean in front of his face with a swipe of his open hand. "I can't tell you I never thought about it. At least what it would be like if he just… disappeared. But that's as far as it went. I may be a degenerate gambler, but I'm not a killer."

"And your brothers? Would one of them take the big step?"

Aaron paused, as if weighing the possibilities. "Not Arnie. He's too much like Dad. But Ayden?" He paused even longer.

"They say still waters run deep," Derek prodded.

"I don't think so. Oh, he'll probably drink a toast celebrating the Old Man's passing when he finally goes, but he's not going to push him. Doesn't have the backbone. At least I don't think he does."

"Anyone else fit the bill?"

Aaron shook his head. "Who knows? Maybe. I'm sure there are people out there who think Dad robbed them blind. There may well be a few he *did* rob blind. But legally. One thing you can say for him, he's no dummy."

"So you have no idea where he is or what happened to him?" It was a Hail Mary pass, but he had to try.

"None. But wherever he is, may he rot in peace."

The interview was over.

"I think that's all the questions I have for right now," Derek said, sliding off the chair to his feet. "Thanks for your time."

"You can show yourself out," Aaron directed, turning his back to the PI to stare out at the turquoise sea just below him.

"I'll let you know if we locate him."

"I'll be sitting on the edge of my chair, waiting for your call."

There was nothing else to say, or ask. So Derek left.

*****

"Oh, great, so now the whole thing may be one sick practical joke?" Brady James asked, his voice echoing tinnily over the speakerphone.

"Might be," Derek said as he swigged a Miller Lite back in his cabin. "But I doubt it."

"Another of those famous DiLaurain hunches?" James asked.

"Something like that. It just seems that there are – or were – a lot of people who didn't particularly like old man Geist, and a few that out-and-out hated him. Usually, that adds up to more than an accidental disappearance."

"You think somebody dumped the old guy overboard?"

"That's what it looks like from here. What about on your end? Learn anything interesting?"

James chuckled. "Quite a group you've got out there."

"So I've noticed. Anything in particular?"

"Well, let's start with the business, Geist & Sons. I contacted an old Post reporter friend who works the Wall Street beat, and he tells me the rumor mill has the company on shaky ground. Seems they've experienced some kind of cash flow problem as of late."

"To the tune of two hundred million dollars," Derek said.

Brady whistled. "That's a pretty big problem. They know who's responsible?"

"Not that I've been able to find out. But they've got a CFO who's an addicted gambler, a CEO who'd just as soon see his father in the ground as in the boardroom, and an entire family pissed off at the Old Man's nurse for getting twenty-five million in his will."

"The gambler – Aaron – have you spoken to him yet?"

"Just finished. Not a big fan of his father either."

"Did he seem particularly upset, or nervous?"

"Not that I noticed. But then again, he was pouring down whiskey like it was… well, whiskey, so I'm not sure I saw the *real* him."

"Picked up on another rumor. Gossip-columnist buddy tells me he's into some very nasty people for something like twenty million in gambling debts."

"Yeh, he admitted as much to me when we talked."

"And he wasn't nervous? If I owed those guys twenty bucks, let alone twenty million, I'd be sweating bullets."

"They're an unusual group, these Geists."

"To say the least."

"Anything on Arnold Jr?"

"Workaholic, pretty good dad as far as attending soccer games and school plays, just enough civic involvement to keep tongues from wagging. One thing – he apparently has one hell of a temper."

"Why do you say that?"

"First, he was arrested back in 1968 for assault. Seems he got into it with another patron at a bar, and the other guy pressed charges."

"Let me guess – no time served."

"Pled down. Community service. Probation for two years."

"What else?"

"This one's not quite as solid, but I got it from a neighbor that his wife almost divorced him a few years back – apparently he mistook her for a punching bag."

"No kidding. Ol' Arnie's a wife beater. Who'd thought?"

"Nothing since then. At least nothing I can find."

"And Ayden? The Mona Lisa brother?"

"Nothing. It's as if he has no existence aside from being a son and brother. Couldn't find a single listing: no Facebook, Twitter, website – nothing. His *kids* have more listings than he does."

"His kids probably have more time to waste. Certainly more than we have."

"Be glad we don't. We have enough problems without taking on the psychoses of the rich."

"I wouldn't mind giving it a try, for a few months anyway."

"So solve the case. Maybe Mrs. Geist will give you twenty-five million."

"Not unless I change her husband's diaper. And that ain't happenin'."

"If you're right, nobody's going to be changing his diaper ever again."

CHAPTER 8

Derek knew that Caroline Earthal and Mrs. Geist would both be awaiting a readout of his interviews, but he decided he preferred Olga's company for a while first.

"So, you find him yet?" she asked when he tracked her down poolside on the upper deck.

"Not yet. Actually, I'm not so sure we will."

"Why?"

The PI looked around to reassure himself no one was close enough to eavesdrop. "I have a funny feeling he went swimming and won't be coming back," he whispered.

"You mean, he dead?"

"I'm afraid so. Of course, unless they recover a body, we'll never know."

Olga re-clasped her bikini top and sat up from the lounger where she'd been working on her tan.

"Someone kill him?"

"Yeh, that's what I'm thinking. Only thing is, half his family had a reason, and the other half didn't seem to give a damn. Leaves a lot of suspects."

"This won't stop our vacation, yes?" she asked with great expectation.

"No! No, of course not," he said, lying through his teeth. If there was one quality anyone who'd spent any time at all with Derek DiLaurain would agree he possessed in spades, it was determination. Once he was on a case, he was on it to the bitter end. But that didn't mean anything would ruin Olga's trip. *Her* vacation would continue as scheduled, with maybe a bit less face time with him. No reason to get excited.

"You can rub suntan oil on my shoulders?" she asked, temporarily mollified.

"My pleasure," he agreed, and he launched into his task with real gusto. As he massaged the oil into her skin, he scanned the decks all around him – a professional habit. It was likely the majority of the Geist clan had gone ashore, but some of them might still be onboard. It took only a few moments to realize that if they were, none of them were hanging by the pool.

"I've got to go talk to the ship's security chief," he announced as he finished his task.

"Okay. I am here for while," she mumbled as she unhooked her top again and lay back down on the lounge.

As much as he wanted to stay, his professional integrity, and personal curiosity, drove him down to the B deck and the ship's security offices.

Miss Earthal was seated at her desk when he muscled open the heavy office door.

"Mr. DiLaurain! Did you catch up with the three brothers?" she asked before he could say a word.

"I did. Quite a group."

"And? Did you learn anything about Mr. Geist's disappearance?"

"Not really, other than that all three of them seem less than heartbroken."

"I'd heard that Mr. Geist Senior was a difficult man to be around."

"If his kids are any indication, he wasn't around often enough to be difficult. Absentee father."

She nodded. "Well, we've got something you might find interesting. Our techs just made available the footage from all 34 security cameras we've got located throughout the ship."

"Has anyone gone through it yet?"

"We only got it about twenty minutes ago. Want to join me in a viewing?"

"I'd love to. Thanks."

She led Derek a few offices down the hallway, to a compact but electronics-filled room where her two assistants and another young man awaited them. They had already started reviewing the tapes.

"Gentlemen – find anything yet?" she asked by way of an introduction.

"Thirty-four varieties of nothing," Todd groaned.

"Like watching paint dry," Eric added.

"You must be DiLaurain," the remaining assistant said, standing – and then bending down – to shake Derek's hand. "I'm Jeff, Woodson. The IT guy onboard."

"Pleased," Derek said, looking past Woodson even as he shook his hand. Behind him was a projected image of all 34 screens, blown up to something like six feet by nine, with a running timecode identifier in the top left-hand corner. "Is that all of them?"

"That's the whole bunch. There are a few areas on the ship where we don't have coverage, but we can see probably 90-95 per cent."

"Anything out of the ordinary so far?"

"We saw the two Geist brothers leave the dinner and go out on-deck, and we followed Mr. & Mrs. Geist from the dining room back to their suite – accompanied by the nurse, of course."

"What about Ayden – the middle son?"

"He and his wife left at about the same time as his parents and headed straight to their cabin."

"Nothing strange with the grandkids?"

"Nothing. As of 8:30 pm, which is how far we've got, everything seems absolutely normal."

"Did you pick up on any leads?" Todd asked him.

"Nah. They're all just one big, happy, dys-functional family. If this was a reality show they'd call it Big Father."

"So we still don't know what happened to Mr. Geist Senior?"

"I don't."

"So what next?" the security chief asked.

"I suppose we look through the rest of the footage, see if anything leaps out."

"Jeff?" Caroline cued.

For the next two hours the four men and their boss reviewed all 34 camera feeds, in fast motion, slow motion, stop motion, and repeatedly, in some sections, at regular speed. What seemed clear was this: after the debacle of the dinner will reading, all the key players made their way back to their rooms, some faster than others. (Aaron made a brief two hour visit to the onboard casino, where he seemed to do little more than break even.) The review team fast-forwarded to a little after midnight, when the action picked up a bit.

First, Aaron, after less than an hour in his cabin, returned to the casino for another stint at the baccarat table. Except for a couple of bathroom breaks, he sat at his table until 2 a.m. Arnie's two sons, Arnold III and

Andrew, snuck out of their family's suite around 12:30 and spent the next hour or so in one of the ship's toney bars, swigging beers and trying (unsuccessfully) to pick up chicks. Their father, Arnold Jr., made a quick visit to Ayden's cabin, staying less than five minutes before returning to his own room.

It was the video feed that included the exterior of the elder Geists' suite that prompted the most animated reaction, however. A few minutes before midnight a waiter exited pushing a cart piled high with glasses and plates, followed almost immediately by another waiter, pushing another cart, who stopped by for a very brief visit before leaving empty-carted. Several minutes passed without any movement. Then…

"Woa! What do we have here?" Eric called out when the door to the suite edged open to reveal Mr. Geist, slouched down in his wheelchair, trademark black glasses outlining his drawn face, his legs covered by a tan blanket and his head covered by a tan knit cap, being pushed by his granddaughter Alma, herself wearing a light blue windbreaker.

"Actually, she told me about taking him on a midnight stroll," Derek admitted. "Sorry."

"And you didn't think to share that piece of information with us?" Todd challenged.

"Got caught-up interviewing the Geist brothers."

"All right, enough," Ms. Earthal intervened. "Let's see where they go."

As the video continued, Alma pushed her grandfather's wheelchair to an elevator at the far end of the hallway and from there up to the top deck, where they wound their way behind the diesel ship's huge smokestack before reappearing on their way to a platform on the far side of the ship, where Alma and her charge sat for the better part of a half-hour. The video quality was less than superb in the dim lighting on-deck, but it seemed clear that – at first – they exchanged the occasional back-and-forth. From the body language it looked like Alma had asked her grandfather more than once if he wanted to go back inside. But Geist waved her off, staring intently at the spectacular night sky or out at the endless black waves. Alma's hair blew freely in the brisk breeze and she repeatedly hugged her jacket closer to her body. Then, at exactly 12:28, Geist's head lolled forward and rested unmoving on his chest, prompting Alma to take him back to his cabin; she immediately set the wheelchair in motion. It took them a good twelve minutes to reappear on the other side of the smokestack, leading Derek and the others to assume they must've stopped and watched… something for the greater part of that time.

They retraced their steps back to the elevator, and then back down to his suite.

There was no further movement outside the suite until roughly 1 am, when a waiter brought an empty cart to the suite, and left a few minutes later with a smattering of plates and trays.

Derek asked that the video be replayed several times.

"Can we find out what the temperature was last night?" he finally asked.

"I'm pretty sure we can," the security chief said. "Why – is it important?"

"Don't know. Probably not. But you never know."

Eric and Todd rolled their eyes at each other behind the PI's back.

"We'll see what we can do," Earthal said, but without much enthusiasm. "Any other ideas or requests?" It was clear they were coming to a roadblock – no one seemed out of place or character on the videos, and no trace of Mr. Geist had turned up after he'd returned to his suite. There was nothing to give them the lead they so desperately needed.

"Anything from the Bermuda police?" Todd asked.

Caroline shook her head. "Nothing. No leads whatsoever. It's as if he just fell off the face of the earth."

"Or off the deck of this ship," Eric said with no trace of levity.

"I'm beginning to think that's exactly what happened."

"But how do we prove it?" Derek asked. "Without a body, or witness, or *something*, we're just spinning our wheels."

"At this point, I need to talk to the Captain, and I'm sure he'll need to talk with corporate back in New York," Ms. Earthal explained. "For the time being, Mr. DiLaurain, let's put our agreement on pause, sort of speak. Is that ok with you?"

"I'm here for a vacation. I have no problem actually relaxing a bit."

"Good. Thank you. We'll let you know if any information comes up. Will you stay onboard or do you intend to get a hotel room on the island as well?" She seemed a tad snitty on that point.

"My girlfriend and I actually enjoy our little cabin. And it's not as if we're well enough off to go renting additional rooms when we've already paid for this one. We'll take an excursion or two, maybe rent a scooter, but otherwise we should be around, yes."

"Good. Enjoy yourself. And remember to be back by 5 pm day after tomorrow – as they say, time and tide wait for no man."

Derek tried not to grimace as he slid out of his chair and, with a nod of the head to his fellow investigators, he left the security office without looking back. Despite his glib words, Derek couldn't help but muse about the disappearance as he walked back down toward his cabin. People don't just disappear, and wheelchairs don't suddenly leap over three-foot-high deck railings. Someone aboard the Princess had some explaining to do.

*****

"I want to go to beach!" Olga said when Derek informed her about the *time-out* in his investigation. "See pink sand!"

She seemed so enthusiastic that he couldn't bring himself to tell her that the so-called pink sand was just a rosy shade of beige, but heck, maybe that would be enough. She'd been 'trapped' onboard the cruise boat for three days now. Even pink–ish sand might do the trick.

He called his taxi connection, Remmy, and by the time he and Olga had packed up their towels and bathing suits, the Toyota van was parked and waiting for them at the bottom of the gangway.

"So, Remmy, where do you suggest we go to see Bermuda's best beaches?" Derek asked as the driver slid open the van door.

"Depend," the cabbie said, his pale blue shorts and "I ♥ John Malkovich" t-shirt contrasted nicely by his green, black and red knit ski-cap. "You want to go to big long beach, beach with big rocks, neighborhood beach, little private beach… Bermuda's got many beaches, man."

"Big, lonnnng beach," Olga answered with a lascivious smile.

"You've got your answer," the PI said as he climbed up into the passenger seat.

"Elbow Beach it is, Boss."

The cab took them past the tourist shops of Dockyard and out along the south shore of the island, past the spectacular coastal scenery they'd witnessed a few hours earlier. After forty minutes or so, Remmy swung into the long, palm-lined entrance to the eponymous resort located right above the spectacular half-mile pink(ish) sand beach. The staff member that met their taxi smiled broadly at Olga as she stepped from the van, but his smile turned to a look of shock, or at least mild surprise, as Derek climbed down from his front seat perch.

"Welcome!" the uniformed hotel greeter announced just before the PI appeared. "Uh, do you have any luggage?" he added just after.

"Nope. Just here to have a nice cold drink and enjoy your lovely beach," Derek said as he took Olga's arm and strolled into the resort lobby. The greeter raised his arm as if to say something, but he apparently decided against it and turned to Remmy with a questioning glance.

"Don't ask me, man," the cab driver said. "I just drive them around."

Derek and Olga made their way through the lobby, down some stairs, and out the back of the building, to where a series of bars and restaurants skirted the beach and the stunning turquoise blue waters of the Atlantic. In their wake they left a chattering scrum of bemused hotel guests, all of whom were wondering if the unusual duo were some kind of celebrities. The two 'celebrities' barely noticed the attention their arrival elicited.

"It is beautiful!" Olga cooed as they stepped out on a patio that looked directly down on the beach. There were perhaps a hundred people dotting the long expanse of sand, the vast majority of them huddled beneath dark blue umbrellas right in front of the resort.

"A drink to celebrate the beginning of our vacation?" Derek asked.

"Champagne?"

"Why not?" the PI laughed. "I've made enough in the last 24 hours to buy us a few cases of the stuff."

He flagged down a waiter and ordered a bottle of Pol Roger Brut after a short discussion about the merits of the various brands. ("If it was beer, I'd know which is the best deal," he told Olga. "But bubbly? They could sell me carbonated olive oil and I wouldn't know." "But *I* would," Olga sniffed.) Derek told the waiter they'd be headed down to a lounger on the sand, and asked him to bring the champagne to them there.

Once at the bottom of the stairs Derek surveyed the available lounge chairs, trying to pick out the perfect locale for their private beach party.

"May I help you?" a pleasant-enough Bermudian wearing the house colors of the resort asked.

"Just trying to find a good spot," Derek muttered.

"Are you staying at the resort?"

Derek looked to Olga, who rubbed her thumb and forefinger together in an internationally recognized gesture. Derek nodded and pulled a wad of bills out of his pocket. "We are for the next hour or two," he said, peeling off a twenty dollar bill. "We need a place to sip our champagne."

The beach assistant glanced around furtively before snatching the bill out of the PI's hand. "Of course, sir," he said loudly. "May I show you to your chairs?"

"Those over there look pretty nice," Derek said, directing his words to Olga. "What do you think?"

"Ideal-ny," she said in Russian.

"Yeh, I think it's pretty idealny too," Derek agreed with a grin. "Show us the way, por favor."

The beach guy knitted his eyebrows, but did as he was asked.

"I think they do not speak Spanish here," Olga whispered.

"Duh," the PI answered, slapping himself on the forehead.

In moments they were settled into their towel-draped chairs, and moments later the original waiter showed up carrying a large silver champagne bucket with his own towel draped over one arm.

"Shall I decork the bottle, sir, or would you like to do it yourself?" the waiter asked.

"I think I can handle it," Derek said, slipping the man another ten. "Thanks."

The waiter gave him a slight bob of the head and headed back upstairs. The tiny PI, whose very presence had already garnered the attention of nearly every conscious sunbather in the vicinity, used the natural stage to good advantage; with a flourish he whipped out the waiter's starched white towel. Cradling the champagne bottle like a newborn baby, he showed it to Olga for her approval.

"Old Russian proverb," she said with a twinkle. "Can't judge vodka by label. Open!"

Derek needed no further motivation. He tore off the foil sealer, untwisted the wire cage holding the cork in place, and with one practiced twist of the wrist sent an explosive stream of pressurized foam shooting across the sand. People nearby actually clapped. Derek took a small bow.

"M'Lady," he said, his British accent more reminiscent of a drunken Cockney bus driver than a sophisticated royal, "your champagne is served."

They touched glasses and sipped the effervescent wine as gentle waves rolled up onto the long expanse of pink-ish beige sand. A light breeze caressed Olga's dark locks. The sun was warm, but not hot. They stared into each other's eyes, a flush rising to their cheeks. It was a perfect moment.

But one fated not to last.

Derek's cellphone rang, the theme from Dragnet raising eyebrows for a dozen yards in every direction.

"Damn!" he yelled as he dug for the phone.

"Don't answer!" Olga pled, but it was too late.

"DiLaurain!" he half-shouted into the mobile.

"Mr. DiLaurain? Derek?" He recognized the voice as Caroline Earthal from the Princess.

"Yes? Caroline?"

"It is. I'm very sorry to bother you…"

"No, it's not a problem," he lied.

"Well, I'm afraid we just got word from the Bermudian authorities: the body of an 'elderly man' has washed up on Cobbler Island."

"Is it Geist?"

"We don't know yet. We need a family member to make the identification. Would you mind accompanying them?"

Part of him felt like telling them they weren't paying him enough for the hassle. But then he remembered that they were – paying him enough.

"Yeh, sure. Who's going to ID him, and where do I meet them?"

"We'd rather not put Mrs. Geist through the whole nasty business, so we've contacted Arnold Jr. He should already be on his way to the morgue at King Edward Hospital in Hamilton."

"Okay. I'm on my way." As he hung up he noticed the frown on Olga's face.

"No. You are not to leave!" she pouted.

"Sorry, baby. They think they found old man Geist."

"He is…?"

"I'm headed to the morgue."

Olga shook her head. "Poor family."

"I don't know how many of them will be heartbroken, but yeh, poor them." He drained his champagne flute. "This should only take an hour or so. The oldest son needs to identify him, and that should be that. For now."

"We can go back to ship and have vacation then?"

He shrugged. "Depends."

"Depend on what?"

"What the coroner says, and what other evidence turns up. And, then too, whether the cruise line and old lady Geist want to keep paying me."

"I hope not."

"Part of me agrees with you. And part wants to know what the hell happened to the old man."

"Don't care what happen."

"Yeh, well, you seem to be in the majority. We'll see." He gave her a quick peck on the lips and headed back upstairs. He stopped at the Men's room to pull on the shirt and long pants he'd thrown into the beach bag. Remmy was waiting for him in the parking lot just beyond the resort reception.

"Where to, Boss?" the Bermudian asked.

"You know the King Edward hospital?"

"Sure thing. Biggest one on the island."

"That's apparently where the morgue is. Let's go."

From the South Road the cab turned left on Point Finger Road and then about a half-mile up on the right, a large, modern hospital building appeared. Or more accurately several buildings, some noticeably older. The main building, a five or six-story concrete and glass structure with a few splashes of local color, looked to be no more than a couple of years old.

"Did they just build this place?" Derek asked as they turned into the entrance.

"Been working on it for years, but only opened a few months back, right," the cabby said.

The PI scrambled out at the entrance portico and was directed by a bemused hospital worker to the morgue in the General Wing. In the small public area of the section, he found Arnie Jr. waiting impatiently.

"Took you long enough," he complained. "Where'd you come from, the other end of the island?"

"Not quite, but I thought it might be more appropriate if I got out of my swimsuit before coming down here."

Arnold Jr. wore a dark blue short-sleeve shirt and khaki trousers. "Nice of you to make the effort," he grumbled.

Just then an older, heavyset black woman came out from an inner sanctum. "Are you here to identify the recently-discovered body?" she asked both men.

"I am," Arnie spoke up.

"And you?" the woman asked Derek.

"I've been hired to investigate a disappearance," he said. "We think this might be the guy who disappeared."

"Understood. My name is Alice Deeds – assistant coroner. Follow me, please." She held the door leading back to a heavily air-conditioned room in back. Nine stainless steel *drawers* covered the far wall.

"Is this it?" Derek asked. He'd imagined a larger facility.

"We have a couple of other places where we can do an autopsy, but we only have 65,000 people on the whole island," the employee explained. "Not that many die under suspicious circumstances."

The stomach-churning smell of chemicals and dead meat made his head pound. Despite all the times he'd found himself in similar surroundings, he'd never acclimated. The Assistant Coroner slid one of the drawers open to reveal the body, covered by a wrinkled white sheet.

"This is our John Doe," she said.

"Where did they find him?" Derek asked.

"From what I understand, some fishermen found the body just outside the reef, off of one of our smaller islands."

Arnie Jr. stood transfixed, staring at the slab without expression or emotion.

"Are you okay" Derek asked him.

"Yeh, yeh I'm okay. Let's get this over with." He walked to the side of the drawer as Deeds pulled back the sheet.

The face was pale and bruised, but it was definitely Geist.

"That's him," Arnie said, staring as if in disbelief. "That's my father."

"Arnold F. Geist?" the woman asked, jotting on a notepad.

"Yeh."

She drew the sheet back up across the dead man's face. "I'm sorry for your loss."

"Thank you. Is there anything else you need from me?"

"Not right now. But I think the local police may want to talk with you."

"Oh? What about?"

"The autopsy revealed a significant amount of triazolam in your father's stomach, along with alcohol."

"What's that – triaz…?"

"It's a sleep medication. More often known as Halcion."

"That's not a big surprise. Dad's had problems sleeping for years."

"It's not the drug, but the amount," the coroner said. "It was roughly 2 mg."

"Is that a lot?"

"It's around four times the normal dose. For a man his age, and in combination with alcohol… Yes, it was a lot."

Arnie stared at the woman. "So, what does that mean?"

"I don't know. But he had water in his lungs, so he was alive when he went overboard. I'm guessing that's what the police will want to talk to you about."

"I see. Okay, well thank you. You have my contact information if you need to get ahold of me?"

"I think the hospital has it, yes."

"May I ask a question?" Derek ventured.

Arnie and Ms. Deeds looked down at him as if just remembering he was in the room. "Yes, certainly," she said.

"What are the chances this was an accidental overdose?"

"Possible," she answered. "But not many people take four pills by mistake."

"Are you saying you think he killed himself?" Geist asked anxiously. The PI understood his concern. If it got out that old man Geist had offed himself not long after $200 million disappeared from the company coffers, a major scandal would no doubt erupt. And scandal was bad for business.

"I'm not saying anything," Deeds answered. "Just presenting the facts. It's up to the police to draw conclusions."

Arnie nodded. "Yeh, of course. We'll have the funeral home get in touch with your office as soon as we know what's what." He didn't wait for further goodbyes but headed straight for the exit.

"Well, what do you think?" he asked Derek as soon as they got out into the hallway.

"You tell me," the PI answered. "Was your father depressed? Was there anything about the business, or his private life, that might have pushed him to take his own life?"

"My father was a tough old son of a bitch," Geist said. "I can't imagine *anything* pushing him over the edge. And I certainly don't know of anything, business or personal, that might have given him reason."

"How tough was he? I mean, could he still get out of the chair by himself?"

"I... I'm not sure. He still had plenty of piss and vinegar, that much I know for sure. But as for getting up without help, you'd better ask the nurse on that one."

"I'll do that."

They walked out the front entrance in thoughtful silence. As soon as they stepped outside, a black Mercedes pulled up to collect him. "What should I do now?" he asked as the driver opened the door for him. "Should I contact the police, or wait for them to get ahold of me?"

"Unless you want to wait around a police station for an hour while they get their act together, I'd give them a call and see if they want to set up an interview."

"Yeh, good idea. Where will you be?"

"I'm off to get my girlfriend, and then we'll probably head back to the ship."

Geist nodded and started to settle into his seat. "If the cops ask me to come in, would you be willing to come along?"

"I think I'm still on your mother's payroll, so sure. But you might want to consider a lawyer as well."

"Lawyer? Why in hell's name would I need a lawyer?"

"If your father didn't kill himself, then there's still a chance that someone did it for him. And that, Mr. Geist, is murder."

CHAPTER 9

Olga had been less than thrilled by the prospect of leaving the beach to return to the ship, but after some sweet-talking she succumbed to Derek's offer of spending 'quality time' in their cabin before dinner. While she was showering, Derek rang Brady back in Virginia.

"They found the body," he said before any greeting.

"Yeh, good to talk with you too," Brady came back.

"Sorry. Thought I was talking to the great Brady James, not his 13 year-old niece."

"I see the cruise hasn't helped your sense of humor any."

"This whole scene is getting to me," Derek admitted. "Everyone disliked the old goat, but none of them seem to have had it in them to knock him off. So what happened? Coroner says he had enough Halcion in his system to put the whole family to sleep."

"Did he kill himself?"

"If so, his eldest son, at least, doesn't know why. Can you see if you can get someone to access his medical records?"

"Access?"

The PI ignored him. "Ask Chesley if he can get ahold of them. And anything else he can find out about the family."

"It's a little out of his jurisdiction, don't you think?" Chez had been known to bend the rules a bit in DC, where as a longtime police detective he had the connections to get almost any information he needed. But for a Bermuda-based case?

"If my memory serves…"

"If pigs could fly," James interrupted.

"…I think Geist lived in DC, or northern Virginia, a number of years ago. Maybe that'll be enough for Chez to hang it on."

"I'll ask. Anything else new?"

"The champagne is damn expensive here on the island."

"You're breaking my heart. How about the truffles? Overpriced too?"

"Very. How about on your end? Pick up on anything?"

"Actually, I hired our little friend Danny from over at the Hart Building to do a bit of moonlighting. He's scanning the family's online presence – Facebook,

Twitter, Blogs… I don't even know all the stuff. But he's doing some kind of automated software search that kicks out any mention of, or by, any of the Geist crew."

"Somehow I doubt old man Geist was much of a Facebook kind of guy."

"You may be surprised. A lot of companies use social media to promote themselves, or their execs. And even if he wasn't online, maybe some of the younger ones were."

"Yeh, worth a shot, I guess. Let me know if you turn up anything."

"How long does the boat stay in Bermuda?"

"Ship. It's a ship."

"I don't care if it's an aircraft carrier. When does it head for the next port?"

"Tomorrow night."

"You thinking of staying on?"

"Olga would have my balls on a platter."

"Small snack."

"Batta boom. You really should head up to the Catskills. I understand they have rest homes up there where you'd be a big hit."

"Aren't you being paid by Mrs. Geist?"

Derek took the change in tone in stride. "I'm 'on hold'. But now that there's a body, maybe I'll go back on the payroll."

"And if you do? Think she'll want you around?"

"Probably. If so, I'll ask for a nice room at one of the swanky resorts so Olga has a place to hang out while I snoop around."

"They can afford it."

"They could probably buy the whole island."

"Even without the $200 million that disappeared?"

"Speaking of which, did you find out anything more about our buddy Aaron?"

"Not much. Just that he's a well-known whale at casinos and racetracks from Monte Carlo to Macau, and everywhere in between. Apparently he's known for winning and losing seven figures in a sitting. But more on the losing side lately, if the rumors are true."

"Was he being squeezed?"

"Not that I've been able to find out. Anyone who lent him money probably figured he'd be good for it."

"Anything on the rest of them?"

"A lot of charities and prep schools and speeches. Nothing out of the ordinary – for billionaires."

"Is anything ordinary for a billionaire?"

"Not 'you and me' ordinary, but yeh, for them it's ordinary."

"As what's-his-name said, 'the rich aren't like you and me.'"

"They're definitely not like you. Pretty definitely not like me either, now that I think of it. And what's-his-name was Fitzgerald."

"Thanks, prof. I'd like to hang around and complete my graduate class in English Lit, but I gotta go tell the Mrs. what's been going on the past few hours. See if I get my fancy resort suite."

"Good luck with that one. If I come up with anything valuable, I'll email it and call."

"Thanks. For all your help I'll try to sneak a few of those little mini booze bottles back to the States for you."

"Always the prince. Oh, and by the way, he was American."

"Geist? I already know that."

"Fitzgerald. When you finish my English Lit class, you should try American Lit. Broaden your horizons."

"Nice talking to you. Say hi to Anne."

"Will do. And Derek, take care. If someone killed Geist, they might be willing to do it again."

The PI's witty riposte died on his lips.

*****

Derek was hoping that Mrs. Geist had already heard about the discovery of her husband's body. Over the years he'd had to tell bad news to plenty of family members, and it wasn't a part of the job he relished.

It soon became obvious that she hadn't heard.

"Any news?" she asked as soon as he was shown into the family suite by Alma.

"Didn't Arnie Jr. call?"

Her face showed she understood the subtext of his question. "No, why?"

"I'm sorry to be the bearer of bad news," the PI said, "but some fishermen discovered your husband's body a few hours ago."

Alma gasped and put a hand to her mouth. Her grandmother patted her on the arm just before she fell limply into an easy chair.

"Are they sure?" the old lady asked.

"Arnie and I were just down at the morgue. It's him all right."

"Were there any indications what happened?" the granddaughter asked.

"Not really. He'd apparently taken some sleeping pills, so they're checking on that."

"He hadn't been sleeping well for several years now," the widow said. "I guess it happens to a lot of people when they get older."

"But he wasn't depressed, or having any problems...?"

The widow's piercing blue eyes swung quickly to the PI. "Why? Do they think it might be suicide? Is that what they think?"

"They haven't ruled anything out yet. I'd guess the local police will be coming around pretty soon. Now that they have the body."

"Where is it?" Mrs. Geist asked. "The body, I mean. Still at the morgue?"

"Arnie said he was going to call a funeral home to move him there."

"I see." Mrs. Geist looked out a rectangular porthole at the turquoise water glimmering in the afternoon sun. "This is going to cause some problems back home."

"With the company?"

She nodded. "Arnie's been running the business for years now, but Arnold was always the face of the company. There's bound to be an impact."

"Nervous investors?"

"That, and probably some scrutiny by the regulators. I think it's customary when a principal dies."

"Will that be a problem?"

"Don't know. Arnold never really let me in on most of the company business. I hope not."

"We're supposed to be leaving tomorrow," Alma interrupted, her voice wavering.

"That will probably not happen," her grand-mother snapped. "There will be details that will need to be taken care of."

"Can't Arnie do that?" the young woman asked. Derek thought she might cry.

"We'll handle it as a family. We always handle things as a family." She looked to her granddaughter, who blinked several times and seemed to regain some self-control.

"Yes, of course," she said.

"Everything will be okay," Mrs. Geist soothed. "We'll get through this." She shared a private moment with her granddaughter, who forced a wan smile.

"I know, Grandma, I know we will."

Derek watched the tableau with a detached eye. One thing was for certain: the widow Geist *was* a tough old bird.

As if she felt his eyes upon her, Mrs. Geist turned back toward the PI. "How about you? What are your plans?"

"I don't know yet. I was waiting to see what you and Ms. Earthal decided before making any."

"Could you be persuaded to stay for a while? Help us sort this thing out?"

"I'd need a place to live once the ship leaves…"

Ida took the hint. "I'm sure we could find you suitable lodging for a few days."

"My girlfriend would want to stay as well, I think."

"Yes, yes, of course. Alma, would you talk to Arnie – ask him to set something up?"

The granddaughter nodded.

"It's settled then. Would you mind acting as the go-between with the local authorities? I have a feeling that's going to be the biggest headache."

"Sure. I've got a contact I met through Ms. Earthal."

"Good. Then, if there's nothing more…"

Derek was more than ready to leave but felt he needed to show a bit of empathy, even if the widow did not seem to need it.

"Will you two be okay?"

Mrs. Geist snorted. "Us? Look, Mr. DiLaurain, my husband was 90 years old. At that age, it was only a matter of time before he died. The only thing that bothers me is this suicide idea. Doesn't seem like him."

"I'm sure the police will look into it thoroughly."

"Well I'm not. That's why we have you. If Arnold killed himself, I want to know."

"I'll do my best."

"You do that."

As Derek left the suite he wondered whether he'd be better off staying onboard the Princess and sailing off into the sunset. He had a feeling that he'd find out soon enough.

*****

Hamilton police headquarters is a stark, five-year-old, five-story building in the center of the city, crowned by a top floor festooned by Greek columns and lots of glass.

"Strange look," Derek said as Remmy dropped him off in front of the building. Chief Inspector Trott had responded enthusiastically to his request to accompany Arnold Jr. for an interview, even suggesting in veiled hints that he might have some new information to share. He was equally sanguine about the PI coming a half-hour earlier than Arnie.

"We should chat," he'd said.

It took the PI a while to catch the eye of the reception person, but once he did he was shown back to the Inspector's office almost immediately.

"Mr. DiLaurain," Trott greeted him as he got up from behind a desk buried beneath papers of all sizes and colors. "Thanks for coming down." Derek was caught off-guard by the friendlier tone, a sea change from their first meeting, He wondered if it was due to the change of setting, or something else.

"Nice digs," Derek said, glancing around. In fact, the office was not much different than hundreds of others he'd visited, but at least it was newer than most.

"Bermuda takes care of its own. So, I understand you've already been over to the morgue."

"I have. Went there with Arnold Jr."

"Did the Coroner tell you about the sleeping pills?"

"She did. But I've got to tell you, from what I've been able to find out over the past couple of days, I'm not sure I buy the suicide theory. Nobody seems to think he had any real problems, and everyone agrees he was the kind of guy more likely to drive other people to kill themselves than do it himself."

The Inspector smiled. "You can say that; I can't. But as a matter of fact, I agree with you. Especially since I just received the Coroner's full report." The way he said it made Derek take notice.

"And? Something unusual?"

"A couple of things. First, the amount of Halcion in his system, although high, wasn't the level of dose we'd expect in a suicide attempt. Usually people take a handful of pills, not just four or five."

Derek nodded. He'd thought much the same.

"Second, we found skin cells under the victim's finger nails."

"Not belonging to Mr. Geist, I take it?"

"It's already on a plane to the States for DNA testing – courtesy of Mr. Geist Junior. Should have results by tomorrow morning. But there was a significant amount of blood mixed in with the skin cells, suggesting some kind of struggle."

"So now you're thinking the old man was pushed?"

Trott lifted his hands in a show of uncertainty. "Could be. Don't want to jump to any conclusions."

"Any leads on who did it – if it was murder?" The PI knew it was unlikely, but he had to ask.

"Not really. I was hoping you might help on that score. I understand you've talked to most of the key players."

"His three sons, the wife and one grand-daughter."

"So? Any ideas?"

"Well, it's clear that he wasn't Mr. Popularity. Just about all of them had some bone to pick with him."

"Any bigger than others?"

"The youngest kid, Aaron, has a bad gambling problem. And a large sum of money seems to be missing from the company coffers. Murders have happened for less."

"How much money?"

"Two hundred million dollars."

The Inspector whistled. "Wow. *I'd* have killed him for that kind of money," he joked.

"Take a number," Derek responded in kind. It was one of the things he liked about dealing with cops: not matter how horrific the circumstances, they always managed to find some humor in the situation.

"Really. Anyone else have a particular grudge?"

"Like I said, all of them had something they didn't like about the guy. But I'm not sure I'd call any of their gripes sufficient motive for murder."

"Apparently someone disagrees with you."

"So it seems."

Just then a cop came in and announced that Mr. Geist had arrived.

"You sure you don't mind sitting through another interview with Arnold Jr?" the Inspector asked.

"I'm getting paid for it. Besides, sometimes it's interesting to see how someone responds to a different set of questions."

"All right then. Let's get him in here."

Arnie looked a good deal more like the CEO he was than the last time the PI had seen him, wearing an expensive Italian-cut suit, $700 shoes, and a watch that was probably worth more than Derek's classic Caddy back home. *'The man knows how to make an impression,'* he thought as he rose to shake Arnie's offered hand.

Inspector Trott was very sympathetic to the elder Geist's loss, and eased him into the interview with just enough fluff and Island pleasantries to make him relax. Then he got down to business.

After grilling him on his father's recent mental and emotional state, he cut to the heart of the investigation.

"Do you know of anyone who might've wanted your father dead?" he asked without prelude.

"I thought you guys were thinking he might have killed himself."

"A possibility. We don't have enough evidence yet to decide one way or the other. So – enemies?"

"As I told Mr. DiLaurain," he began, turning to look at the PI seated in the chair next to him, "anyone who gets to my father's level in business is bound to have enemies."

"Enemies who wanted him dead?"

"No, not really. Not that I know of, anyway."

"What about this missing two-hundred million I'm hearing about?"

Derek thought Arnie shot him a venomous look, but he might have been projecting.

"We're looking into it."

"I understand your brother has a gambling problem."

This time the glance was real. "I don't see how the two are related," Geist said, his voice taut.

"I don't think the Inspector is saying they are," Derek interceded.

"Not necessarily," Trott agreed. "But you've got to admit, it's an interesting coincidence."

"It *is* a coincidence."

"And you know this how?"

"Aaron has been our CFO for over twenty years, and we've never had a problem with our books. He's always covered his gambling debts himself, and I have every reason to believe he still is. Besides, I very much doubt even Aaron can run up a $200 million debt."

"You'd be surprised what people can do," the Inspector said. "But let's assume you're right. Who then, had a reason to kill your father?"

"I don't know. Maybe it was someone trying to rob him, or maybe it was an accident, or... I don't know. But I don't think anyone close to him would do such a thing."

"Okay. But let's stay with the business. Other than the missing $200 million, how're things going?"

"Good. Very good, in fact. Although it's not common knowledge yet," – he said the last with a lowered voice in hunch-shouldered secrecy – "we've been approached by a larger company about a buy-out. It looks good."

"So there's nothing on the financial end that might have been bothering him?"

"Not that I'm aware of."

Trott nodded while looking up from his notes. "Is there anything else you want to tell me – anything that might help our investigation?"

"Just that all this is as much a mystery to me and our family as it is to you. It doesn't make sense."

"No, I have to agree with you there. But we'll keep looking. With any luck we'll find something to help bring all of you some closure."

"Appreciate that, Inspector," Geist said, standing. "Are we free to leave the Island?"

"I don't see why not. But make sure we have a way of getting in touch with you. All right?"

"Will do. And thank you."

The two men shook, and Derek followed them out of the Inspector's office.

"Well, I guess this pretty much ends your investigation as well," Geist said when he and the PI were alone in front of the police headquarters.

"Might. But your mother wanted me to hang around a bit – help out with settling some of the details."

"I don't see what you can do that my brothers and I can't take care of."

"That's up to her. Maybe what she's hoping for is an explanation of what happened."

"You think you can do better than the local cops on that one?"

"They have a dozen cases they're working. I have just one."

"All right," he said with a distracted look. "Good luck to you." They shook hands.

As the limo drove away, Derek wondered if Arnie shared his determination.

*****

"What's your sense of things with the police?" Mrs. Geist asked. She sat by an open window in the living room of her shipboard suite, with Alma standing just behind her like a faithful servant, or watchdog.

"They'll do their best, I'm sure."

"But...?"

"But, they probably have a lot of cases, and I doubt they have unlimited resources."

"Then you're not hopeful?"

"I really don't know. Depends a lot on the results of the DNA test, I expect."

"DNA test? What DNA test?" Alma asked.

"Didn't Arnie tell you? The Coroner found traces of skin and blood under your grandfather's fingernails. Arnie paid to have them flown to the States for testing."

"How long will that take?"

"Not long. I expect to get word tomorrow."

"What will that tell us?" the widow Geist asked. "I mean, he might have scratched his nurse while she was helping him get into the wheelchair, or a dozen other ways."

"True. But it's all we've got at the moment."

She nodded thoughtfully. "Yes, well, I suppose that's true. Have you seen your new accommodations yet?"

"Didn't know I had any."

"You were off the ship," Alma explained. "I left word with your girlfriend. Olga, is it?"

"It is. What's the name of the place?"

"Arnie likes the Coral Queen," Ida explained, "so we're all moving out there. Except for Aaron, of course."

"Of course," Alma muttered.

"Just one big happy family, huh?" the PI said.

"Not so happy," Mrs. Geist said. "Not so happy at all."

"No, of course not. Sorry about that."

"It's our problem, not yours." For a moment there was a tense silence. "So, we'll talk further at the resort."

"Right. See you there."

As he left the suite, Derek couldn't help but wonder if a member of that big happy family had dumped the old man overboard. If one did, which of them – if any – really wanted to know the truth?

*****

"But I want spend more time with *you*!" Olga wailed when he told her about the new arrangement.

"We'll have time; I promise. It'll just be a few days getting things settled, and then we'll either stay here for another week, or pick up the next cruise coming through. How's that sound?"

She sat on the edge of their bed, pouting. "Okay."

"It could be worse. You liked the Coral Queen, right?"

"Pool is nice."

"There, see? We'll spend a few days at the resort, you can hang out at the pool, and whenever I'm back we can… get to know each other again." His leer was classic DiLaurain.

"I want know you *now*," she said as she pulled his head to the gentle valley between her mountainous breasts.

"I think that can be arranged," he said, though it sounded more like "Ah thin thot con be range," through the muffling caress. It didn't matter. She got the message.

****

By the time they'd finished their extracurricular activities, showered, and packed, it was nearly sundown. Remmy ran them over to the Coral Queen, where they were quickly ensconced in a junior suite that featured its own patio and miniature soak pool, wet bar, a Jacuzzi tub, two 60" flat screens, and a bed so large the tiny PI virtually disappeared in its lavender satin sheets.

As soon as he got Olga set-up watching a Russian-language movie on pay TV, Derek plunked himself down next to the pool and called Brady in Virginia.

"Got anything for me?" he asked before even saying hello.

"Yeh, good to talk to you too," the ex-reporter said. "As a matter of fact, I do."

"And?"

"And, our friend Chez has been hard at work. It seems your little Miss Alma is not quite the choir girl she would appear."

"In what way?"

"Back about fifteen years ago she was arrested. Three times, in fact."

"Alma?" He could barely believe it. "For what?"

"First time was when she was 15 – for shoplifting. She 'forgot' to pay for a cellphone."

"Could happen, I suppose. Then?"

"Then, the next year, she was busted for possession of pot."

"Sales or just personal use?"

"Three point four ounces. Could've been either, but she got off with a slap on the wrist."

"I'd imagine her family got her some big ticket lawyers."

"I'd imagine. But just a few months later she spent a short time in the can."

"For what?"

"Solicitation."

"What?!" It couldn't be. Alma, a hooker? "Are you sure you got the right Alma Geist?"

"Oh, I'm sure all right. Had to sweet-talk a clerk at the courthouse in Indianapolis to even see the paperwork. They managed to get the records sealed."

"No kidding. Man, I wouldn't have guessed that in a million years."

"Looks can be deceiving."

"Don't I know it. Anything else? Any later charges or convictions?"

"Nope. As far as the legal system is concerned, she fell off the face of the earth after she turned 18. Not so much as a parking ticket that Chez could find."

"I'm not sure how or if that helps us down here, but it *is* interesting. How about the others?"

"Nothing much. One DUI for your gambler."

"Aaron?"

"He's the youngest one?"

"That's him. No big surprise. Did Chez find out anything about the old man's medical conditions?"

"Nothing of extreme interest. He was old. Had the kinds of problems old people get."

"Was he prescribed Halcion?"

"He was." Derek could hear his friend shuffle through some papers. "A Doctor Silverstein put him on the stuff after he started having troubles sleeping. Been taking it for nearly two years."

"I thought that stuff was habit-forming."

"I guess they didn't figure he'd live long enough to develop much of an addiction."

"They were right."

"Unfortunately for him."

Derek flipped up his shades as the daylight faded to a pale pinkish-orange smudge on the distant horizon. "Have you heard anything from Danny-boy?"

"Not yet. Got an email from him that said he expects to get something by mid-day tomorrow. I'll give you a call as soon as I hear."

"Great. Thanks."

"How's the weather out there?"

"Your basic 75 degrees with a light breeze. I saw it's getting chilly in DC."

"Dropped into the 40's last night. Anne had the heat turned up to 80."

"You should bring her out here. You'd like it – both of you."

"Only if your close personal friends the Geists pick up the tab – tell 'em you need a second set of eyes."

"To see what? So far, all I'm doing is running around in circles."

"Like I said, you need another set of eyes. So, no new theories?"

"Just a lot of maybes. Think I'll go have a chat with little Miss Alma. See if her 'bad girl' period can shed any light on this screw-up."

"Sounds like a stretch."

"Stretching is something I'm used to. Coming up against a blank wall is not."

"Well, just keep plugging. Like I always say…"

"Getting the story is four parts shoe-leather and one part genius. I know."

"Must've mentioned it before."

"Not more than a couple thousand times."

"Then maybe it's started to sink in."

"Aren't you the wild-eyed optimist."

"Wild-eyed, occasionally. Optimist?"

"I know: a stretch. Okay then, we'll talk when we talk."

"Stay safe."

Derek chuckled? In Bermuda? What could possibly happen in Bermuda?

CHAPTER 10

When Derek called the front desk to talk to Alma, he learned that they still hadn't left the Princess and weren't expected until later that evening. He called the ship to be sure and was connected directly to Mrs. Geist.

"Mrs. Geist!" he said when he heard the unexpected voice answer the phone. "I was calling for Alma."

"She's talking with the ship's people, getting us ready for the move. Is there something I can help you with?"

"I thought the Princess was leaving at 5."

"They were kind enough to postpone their departure for two hours so we could finish packing. We've been... preoccupied."

"Yeh, I can imagine."

"So, can I help you with something?"

He debated asking her about the granddaughter, but decided against it, both for ethical reasons (he tried not to divulge personal information unless absolutely necessary) and more practical considerations (he wasn't at all sure the young woman would speak freely with the old lady leaning over her shoulder.)

"No, not really. If you'd just tell Alma to let me know when she has some time?"

"Will do. We should be over at the Coral Queen in an hour or so. But she may be a little busy getting us settled at first."

"I understand. No rush. Just have her call when she can." In fact, there *was* a rush, but he wasn't about to tell the grandmother that.

When he hung up, he marveled – not for the first time – at the clout wielded by the ultra-wealthy. He could just imagine what they'd say if *he* had asked to delay the departure of the entire ship so that he could have a little extra time to pack. No chance on earth.

He thought about kicking off his shoes and hanging around the suite until the Geists made the move to the resort, but with Olga already happily occupied he decided to use the time to good advantage. He had a few more questions for Mr. CFO. He called the Hibiscus to make sure the youngest son was available.

"Again? You want to talk to me again?" Aaron asked when the PI made his request. "What for? Has something changed?"

"I'd just like to clarify a few things."

"So ask."

Derek hesitated. He always liked to interview face-to-face. It was too easy to lie to a hunk of plastic and circuits, and too difficult to discern when those lies took place. No, he liked to watch the eyes dart, the lips get dry, the sweat start to drip down the side of the face. That's how he knew they were BS'ing him.

"If you don't mind, I think it'd be… mutually beneficial if I talked to you in person. It won't take long, only fifteen minutes or so." He liked that one: 'mutually beneficial.' He'd have to remember it for next time.

"For Christ's sake," Aaron mumbled. "Okay, all right. Come on over. But just fifteen minutes. I've got better things to do than chat with a midg… PI."

The pause lasted just an instant, but Derek heard it, and he could guess what Aaron had almost said. It didn't matter. He'd heard the same, and worse, a million times before.

Derek tried to get ahold of Remmy, but he didn't answer his cellphone so the PI jumped in a cab that was waiting by the front entrance.

"Where to?" the driver asked.

"Hibiscus."

"No problem. Have you there in no time."

This driver wasn't as affable and outgoing as Remmy, but Derek was lost in his own thoughts anyway, so conversation was neither needed nor expected. They drove in near-silence for about five minutes, the only sound the hum of the tires on the pavement, when Derek noticed the roar of a motorcycle passing on his right. He glanced up to see what kind of bike put out such a deep-throated growl, but what he saw snapped him out of his reverie and sent him diving to the seat: Gun!

Two loud explosions sent shards of glass showering over the seat as the driver slammed on his brakes and fishtailed to a shuddering stop.

"What the hell was that?!" the driver shouted.

Derek strained to make out a license number on the quickly accelerating bike, but it was moving too fast and was too far away to see in the dim twilight.

"Looks like either you or I pissed some people off," the PI said as he brushed glass from his hair. It took a while, but he persuaded the driver to continue on to the Hibiscus. A smarter man, perhaps a saner man, would've considered going back to his suite, or maybe even going home. Derek never gave it a moment's thought.

*****

"They *what*?!" Aaron yelled when Derek told him about the 'road incident.'

"Shot at us. Twice," the PI said.

"Seems you rub people the wrong way."

"Occupational hazard. You don't happen to have a beer, do you?"

"You're not going to turn this into a drunken blab-athon are you?"

"Nope. Just ask my questions, drain my beer, and I'll be gone."

Aaron didn't look entirely convinced, but he probably hoped to get more gory details of the shooting. "Hey, Edie, do we have any more beer in the frig?" he called out to the emptiness of his suite.

"Hold on – let me check," a familiar female voice answered from one of the bedrooms. Just a few seconds later the same woman Derek had seen earlier sunning herself out back strolled toward the kitchen. She'd changed into a thin white cotton sun suit since last he'd seen her.

"Any idea who shot at you?" Aaron asked, his demeanor cool and controlled once again.

"Nope. Probably some local thug who needed a hundred bucks for some pot."

"Pot? How does he get pot by shooting at you?"

"I assume someone paid him," Derek said as he examined an impressionist bronze fish statue that sat on a shelf next to the monstrous wall-mount TV.

"Why? Any ideas?"

"I don't know. Maybe somebody didn't want me asking questions about your father's death. Speaking of which, did you tell anyone I was coming over here?"

Aaron's expression went from surprised, to shocked, to angry – all within a couple of seconds.

"You don't think *I* had anything to do with this, do you? That's crazy!"

"You were the only one who knew I was coming this way."

"There are only three main roads on this whole island. Anyone who had a bone to pick with you could figure out how to get to you in five minutes."

"True. Just seems quite a coincidence that it happened a few minutes after I hung up with you."

"That's all it was – a coincidence."

At that moment, his attractive young friend returned from her errand, a cold Sam Adams in hand.

"Couldn't find a mug, so I brought the bottle," she said.

"Thanks. Bottle's fine," Derek smiled.

She eyed him without a hint of self-consciousness. "You're kind'uv short," she said.

"That might be the nicest thing anyone's said to me all day."

"He's had a tough day," Aaron interpreted. "Someone took a shot at him."

"With a gun?"

"Only way to do it."

"Are you hurt?" she asked, genuinely concerned.

"Just my feelings. And after I finish this nectar of the gods, those will be doin' a lot better as well."

"'Nectar of the gods,'" she said with a chuckle. "That's cute."

"You're kind'uv cute yourself."

"All right, all right, enough with the mutual admiration society," Aaron complained. "You have some questions for me?"

"That's my cue," Edie said, turning to leave.

Derek watched her sashay across the tile floor, her high heels clicking like a ball-peen hammer metronome.

"Hello? Can we get on with this?" the youngest Geist brother interrupted his reverie.

"Huh? Yeh, sure, no problem." The PI took a big swig of his beer and scurried up on a leather couch.

"I was hoping you might be able to give me a little background on Arnie's daughter, Alma."

"Alma? Why didn't you ask Arnie?"

"Because I want the truth. And fathers don't always tell the truth about their own kids."

"I don't understand."

"My colleagues back in the States have been doing some investigating into the Geist clan – looking for anything that might help explain your father's

disappearance and death. They came across some…
unexpected behavior on the part of your niece."

The tension in Aaron's eyes disappeared. "Oh, I
get it, you're talking about her brush with the law – is
that it?"

"Brush-es" Derek corrected.

"More than one? I knew about the shoplifting, but
I didn't realize there was another one."

"*Two* others, that we've been able to find."

"For what?"

"Possession of marijuana, and …" He hesitated.
Personal information was inviolate, except when he
needed answers. Like now. "… solicitation."

Geist's face fell. "I don't understand."

"They caught Alma with enough pot to warrant a
felony arrest, and about a year later they busted her for
prostitution."

Aaron looked as if someone had hit him between
the eyes with a 2 x 4. "That's impossible."

"I'm afraid it's not. We accessed her court
records."

"But… why… I mean, she had everything she
could possibly need. And that's not her. Not Alma at
all."

"That's what I thought. Any idea why the sudden
change? Any family rumors about boyfriend troubles, or
school bullying? Anything?"

"No! Nothing that would cause something like *that*. It's completely out of character."

"Were you two close? Close enough that you would've known?"

Geist shook his head sadly. "Do you have any kids, or nephews, nieces?" he asked, his voice low.

"Not yet."

"Yeh, well if you ever do, make time for them while they're still young enough to want to spend time with you." He fidgeted with a shirt button. "I guess I figured I'd have plenty of time to get to know my brothers' kids, but by the time I got around to it, they were all grown and had their own lives. At this point I'm just the crazy black sheep uncle with some bad habits."

"That bother you?"

He grunted bitterly. "What is this, a shrink session?" He waited for an answer that didn't come. "Yeh, I guess it does," he continued. "I'm not going to tell you I'm losing sleep over it, but if I could do it over again, yeh, I'd try to spend some more time with them when they were little."

"Who did know her?"

"I'm not really sure. I suppose my father and mother knew her best. At least she was always over there at their summer house when school got out."

"Did all the grandkids spend summers with your parents?"

He shrugged. "You're asking the wrong guy, remember? But from what I recall, she spent the most time with them. They all went over there, but I don't think any of the others stayed for an extended period every summer like she did."

"How about the nurse, Ms. Cruz? What's the scuttlebutt on her?"

"A pretty nice butt, actually," he smiled. "But Daddy always liked a nice butt."

"Did he?" Something new.

"What, none of the others mentioned Dad's... friendships?"

"Not really. Why don't you tell me about them."

"Not much to tell, really. He worked a lot, and when he had free time I guess he wanted what he wanted, when he wanted it."

"And so there were women?"

"Some. I was a kid. But I remember my mother giving it to him good a few times."

"About other women?"

"Among other things. But yes, about women."

"Why didn't she leave?"

"It was a different time. And she had us kids."

"So she toughed it out."

"She toughed it out, and made it tough on him whenever he was around. That's probably one reason why he wasn't around much."

"But surely he wasn't fooling around with Ms. Cruz – not at 90?!"

"Who knows? Doubtful, but I wouldn't put anything past that old bastard."

"Okay. Change of direction: the $200 million. Where'd it go?"

Sometimes Derek could see the impact of a question even before the person opened their mouth. This was one such occasion.

"I don't know. Whoever moved it knew what they were doing. They shuffled it through a half-dozen subsidiaries, off-shore holdings, you name it. But we'll find out."

"Any ideas?"

"Who did it? Nah. Could've been anyone."

"Really? *Anyone* could've moved $200 million out of your company's accounts without sounding alarm bells? Arnie told me you were a smart guy – doesn't sound that way."

Derek expected to get a rise out of the CFO. What he got surprised him.

"Arnie said that?" He looked thrilled.

"Surprised?"

"A little. Like I said, I'm the black sheep."

"Well, he apparently sees through that disguise. But back to the two hundred million – how many people had access to that kind of money in your company?"

"Officially? Not many. Really just my father, Arnie and me. But in this day and age, anyone with a laptop and a head for hacking could've pulled it off."

"So you have indications that it was an outside job?"

"Not really... What the hell's this gotta do with the old man's death, anyway?"

"Two hundred million is a lot of motivation."

"You think my father found out someone was stealing from the company and they killed him to keep him quiet?" He sounded incredulous.

"As good as any other theory I've heard."

"That would pretty much narrow the possible suspects to Arnie and me, right?"

"If the money was taken by someone inside."

"And he's the Chamber of Commerce CEO while I'm the playboy gambler. Doesn't look good for me."

"Doesn't it?"

Aaron stared at the PI, then down at his watch. "Your fifteen minutes are up, Mr. DiLaurain."

"One last question," Derek insisted.

"Make it fast."

"Your mother – you said she made things tough for him. How bad was it?"

"Jesus. You guys'll suspect anyone, won't you?"

"That's who commits murders, Mr. Geist – anyone."

Aaron took a deep breath. "It was worse ten, fifteen years ago. It's been pretty good between them for the past few years. Hell, they went on a half-dozen stupid cruises together."

"And look how that turned out."

With that, the interview was most definitely over. As he made his way back to the reception desk, Derek re-ran the discussion in his head. Aaron had boiled it all down to the bare bones: if the old man's death was somehow linked to the missing money, it didn't look good for him. Yet the PI couldn't help but think that the youngest Geist son had been telling the truth. Call it a gut feeling, intuition, professional hunch – whatever. He didn't strike the PI as the lying kind.

Which left Arnie.

*****

Arnold Jr. was not particularly enthusiastic about talking to the PI again at 8 o'clock at night, but Derek was his usual persuasive self and the company CEO relented. Grudgingly.

"Do we really have to do this now?" he asked when he answered Derek's knock on the suite door.

"It'd be better, for you and for me."

Arnie didn't look convinced, but he let the PI in anyway.

"This better be good."

"Actually, I think it may be bad."

The elder son stopped in mid-stride. "What now? Has somebody else disappeared?"

"Not yet. But I've got some questions that you might find... troubling."

"About?"

Derek motioned to the sofa behind him. "May I sit down?"

"Yeh, yeh, of course. Have a seat. Can I get you anything to drink?"

Just then, Brenda came out from wherever she'd been hiding. "Mr. DiLaurain! Didn't expect to see you again so soon."

"This place is just too inviting," the PI said. "And the clientele too."

She smiled at his little joke. "I bet you're a terror with the women."

"Just a fright, at least on a good day."

"Honey, Mr. DiLaurain and I have things to discuss..."

"Oh, yes, certainly," she said, taking the hint with as much grace as could be expected. "Can I get you anything?"

"I've already asked him, believe it or not," Arnie said, turning to Derek. "So – what'll it be?"

"A beer, if you've got one."

"I think we do," Arnie said as he headed for the kitchen fridge.

"I can get that," his wife waved him off. "You two make yourselves comfortable. Want anything, hon?"

"No, no I'm fine, thanks Bren." He sat uncomfortably across from the PI in his leather easy chair. "Okay, so what's all this about?"

Derek glanced over in the direction of Arnie's wife, and waited patiently until she delivered his beer.

"Thanks."

"My pleasure. I'll leave you two boys alone. I have a tasteless and poorly-written romance novel to finish." She smiled and Derek smiled back.

"Nice woman," he said when she'd left the room.

"*I* think so. Now, about my father, or whatever it is you want to talk about?"

Derek took out his notebook, more for show than a desire to jot quotes. "Well, first off, I wanted to let you know that some guy on a motorcycle took a shot at me about an hour ago – two shots, actually."

Arnie stared at him as if he'd lost his mind. "*Shot* at you? Here, in Bermuda?"

"Just down the road a ways. Some guy in black leathers, wearing a black helmet."

"My god… You weren't hurt?"

"No, but a window on the cab will need to be replaced."

"Who would do such a thing?"

"You don't have any ideas?"

Arnie's eyes narrowed. "Are you suggesting that *I* might have had something to do with that?"

"I'm not suggesting anything. But I gotta think that it wasn't just a random drive-by. So it probably has something to do with your father's death."

"Maybe so, but I don't know a damn thing about it."

"Okay, good. I didn't really think you did, but I thought you'd want to know."

"So now I know," he said petulantly. "What else?"

Derek made a grand show of flipping through his notes, stopping at some random scribbling as if it demanded his attention.

"The missing money," he began.

"What money? Oh, you mean the $200 million."

"Is there more money missing?"

"No! At least not that I'm aware of. Do you know something?"

"I don't. But when I talked to your brother…"

"Which one?"

"Aaron. He said only you, your father and he had legitimate access to that kind of money in the company. Is that right?"

"Ah. So now you're thinking either Aaron or I pushed him off the ship to hide the missing money."

"Did you?"

Arnie looked disgusted. "Do you actually get paid to come up with this crap?"

"Sometimes. Did you have anything to do with the missing $200 million?"

"No." No explanation, no offended outrage. Just no.

"Okay. Do you know *anything* about the missing money?"

"Didn't we just go through all this yesterday?"

"Just checking to see if anything's changed since then."

"Well nothing has changed. You're still as annoying as ever, and I still don't know what happened to the money or what happened to my father. Now, do you have anything else, or is that about it for today's harassment?"

"Your daughter, Alma – she had a rough time when she was a teenager, didn't she?"

Her father stared, his face cold and hard. "What does that have to do with anything?"

"I don't know. I only know that when something completely unexpected turns up in an investigation, it usually pays to track it down."

"Well this time it doesn't."

"She was arrested three times, is that right?" Derek went on, ignoring Arnie's anger.

"I said…"

"Why? Why does a good girl from a good family suddenly have problems with the law? Usually, there's some underlying reason. Was she having trouble in school? At home?"

For a moment Derek thought the elder Geist would explode, but then he turned his head away and exhaled, long and slow.

"No, she didn't have any problems at home, or in school. At least not at first," he said evenly.

"What reasons did she give? I mean, you must've asked her what was going on, right?"

"We asked. We got her professional help. We did everything we could think of."

"But she never revealed the problem?"

"No. And then, one day it was over. She was back to being the wonderful young woman we knew her to be."

"When was that?"

"Just after her 18th birthday."

"So, what changed?"

"I don't know. The only thing we could see was that she moved out, went away to college."

"Sounds like everything wasn't hunky-dory at home."

"She claimed it wasn't that. Said she'd just moved beyond it."

"And you took that at face value?"

"Look," Arnie said, leaning forward as if to close the physical as well as emotional distance between interviewer and interviewed, "she was happy. She got good grades, had good friends."

"So why rock the boat – was that it?"

The wrinkles at the corners of his eyes flexed. "Something like that, yes. But what could her troubles possibly have to do with your investigation? To be blunt, it seems to me you're just fishing, snooping around in other people's lives for the hell of it."

Derek smiled. "Hate to tell you, Arnie. But you guys aren't all that interesting. If what I wanted was to see weirdoes doing weird things, I'd watch reality TV."

"So why then?" He was serious, concerned. Derek felt a pang of empathy for the poor guy.

"Like I said, I need to track down every loose thread. It might mean nothing. Then again…"

"It doesn't. It couldn't."

"You may be right. You probably are. But I've got to do my job, and in my line of work, nothing is ruled out until the case is closed."

"I see. Must be pretty depressing sometimes."

"Sometimes. But then again, when you unravel a tightly wound ball of string and get to the heart of a case, you get a feeling of satisfaction that makes it all seem worthwhile."

"I hope you get that feeling in this case, Mr. DiLaurain."

"So do I, Arnie. So do I."

CHAPTER 11

Derek had paid the desk clerk twenty bucks to let him know when Mrs. Geist and her granddaughter checked-in to the Coral Queen. He was sipping a cold one, watching a Redskins game on TV while waiting for Olga to get out of the shower, when the phone rang.

"They just went to their room," the desk clerk said in a conspiratorial whisper.

Derek thanked him and yelled to Olga that he had to run out for a few minutes; he ignored her Russian invective. He was sufficiently familiar with the grounds of the Queen that he found his way to the Geist suite without any problems. He'd considered calling them first to give them a heads-up he was coming over, but decided that the surprise might facilitate more truthful responses.

"Mr. DiLaurain!" Alma said with an expression that was definitely more shock than welcome.

"May I come in?" he asked.

"I... Let me check," the young woman said as she partially closed the door and stepped back inside.

"Grandma!" she yelled, "Mr. DiLaurain is here. Can he come in?"

"Doesn't that man ever call it a day?" the older woman called back. "Okay, let him in. I'll be there in a minute."

Alma reopened the door with a smile. "Come on in. Grandma will be with us in a minute."

Derek tried to study her out of the corner of his eye as he slipped past; she didn't seem particularly worried or nervous.

"Can I get you anything?" she asked.

"Got a beer?"

"Let me take a look in the mini-bar. Have a seat – I'll be right back."

As she headed to the wet bar, he made himself comfortable on the massive leather sofa that took up most of one wall in the living room. He thought he probably looked like an overstuffed Disney-character cushion perched on the huge couch, but he'd long since stopped worrying what other people thought about his appearance. He noticed, of course, but care? Nah.

"Here you go," Alma said after a short delay, carrying a dark bottle with a golden label he recognized at thirty feet. "I hope Dos Equis will do." She pronounced Equis as if it were a part of a horse, but the PI got the idea.

"Love it. I once flew down to the Yucatan just to see the Mayan pyramids and drink cases of this stuff. I still remember that trip. At least parts of it."

"I'm afraid we only have a few bottles," she teased.

"Should be enough. Unless you and your grandmother tell some really long stories."

"We'll try to keep to the point."

"Mr. DiLaurain!" Ida Geist interrupted, strolling into the living room. "So good to see you again." If he hadn't overheard her comment to the granddaughter moments earlier, he might have actually believed the old lady.

She came over to where he was perched on the sofa and waved him off when he feinted at getting up to greet her. "Stay right there. I can still bend that far."

"Mrs. Geist. I apologize for stopping by at this late hour."

"Don't be silly," she lied, "it's not an imposition at all." She sat in the largest of the two easy chairs facing the sofa. "So, what's behind this unexpected pleasure?"

He'd given them sufficient advance warning before they ever left the Princess so he struggled to understand how his presence could be unexpected, but he kept his puzzlement to himself.

"Have you spoken with any of your sons?"

"No, should I?"

"Someone took a couple of shots at me while I was taking a cab over to see Aaron," he said. "Didn't hit me but did a pretty good job on a side window."

"What?!" the older Geist said, holding her hand to her mouth. Derek couldn't help but think the move seemed out of character for the tough old bird.

"That's terrible!" Alma shouted in near-harmony. "Did you see who shot at you?"

"Not really. He was all in black – leathers, helmet – but he was small and riding a fast bike. Neither of you would know anything about that, would you?"

"Are you suggesting…?" Mrs Geist began, as offended as if he'd accused her of wearing costume jewelry and off-the-rack outfits.

"I asked Arnie and Aaron; had to ask you two as well."

"Well I most assuredly don't know anything about who shot at you," Ida went on, her voice not an iota more forgiving.

"Neither do I," Alma chimed-in, with a great deal less emotion.

"I didn't think so. But as I said, had to ask. May I ask a few other questions?"

"Will they be as offensive as your first few?" The old lady stared at him without a hint of a smile.

"Probably not. But sometimes I don't see my questions in the same light as the people I'm asking."

"Evidently... Well, since you're already here, you may as well ask. That way perhaps we won't have the *pleasure* of your company again tomorrow night."

"My loss, I'm sure." He held his grin even in the face of Ida's withering grimace. "So – the missing $200 million: I've been told only Arnie, Aaron and your late husband had ready access to it. Is that your understanding as well?"

"I don't know much about the workings of the company," Alma said.

"Didn't expect you to. Mrs. Geist?"

The elderly woman hesitated, then responded obliquely. "I... I didn't have direct access, if that's what you mean."

"Indirect?"

"If you count my husband's access as my indirect access, then yes. But that's a stretch."

"Did anyone else have that kind of control over the money?" Derek pushed.

"Not that I was aware of," Mrs. Geist said.

"Okay," the PI said, looking at his prop notebook to set the stage, "now I'd like to ask a few questions that are a little... personal. Would that be all right?"

"Personal in what way?" Ida asked.

"Well, for example, my investigation has turned up the fact that you, Alma, had some brushes with the law back in your teen years."

"That was a long time ago!" the young woman bleated. "I was just a kid!"

"And what in God's name does that have to do with Arnold's death?" her grandmother asked, her face and tone as cold as winter in Green Bay.

"I don't know. Do you?"

Ida stared Derek straight in the eyes, daring him to continue along those lines of questioning. But out of the corner of his eye, the PI thought he saw her granddaughter turn to her with a look that might have been surprise, or confusion, or...?

"We have no idea what you're talking about. And I'm beginning to think you don't either," Mrs. Geist said.

"Alma? No idea?" Derek asked, undaunted.

"I... uh... No! No idea!" she answered. He could hear the quiver in her voice. *What the hell?* he wondered.

"That's quite enough, Mr. DiLaurain!" Ida ordered. "I hired you to find my missing husband, not to browbeat our family members!"

"My apologies. I was under the impression you wanted to find out how he died."

"Of course I want to know how he died," she said, her self-control returning, "but I don't see how grilling my granddaughter over a few indiscretions committed years ago will help accomplish that goal."

Derek struggled with his own self-control. "Do you have any idea how many cases I've worked on over the last twenty years or so, Mrs. Geist?"

"I have no clue," she answered. She didn't seem to have any interest, either.

"Hundreds. And one thing I've learned during that time is that people are generally predictable: good people usually remain good people, and bad people usually remain bad people. So when there's a change in that pattern – when good people suddenly do bad things, and then go back to being good people again, for example – (he glanced over at Alma), it makes me wonder."

"Well wonder somewhere else. I won't have you upsetting my granddaughter, especially not after she just lost her grandfather."

Derek nodded his acquiescence. It was clear he'd have to get the information some other way.

"All right. Then how about a couple of questions about that night?"

"If they pertain to my husband's disappearance, go ahead."

"The security video on the ship captured you, Alma, taking your grandfather up to the top deck for some air right around midnight. Is that right?"

"We already talked about that," Alma said.

"Yes, we did. But what I wanted to find out is whether either of you saw, or heard, Mr. Geist leave the suite later that night."

"I didn't," Ida said, adding: "Arnold and I slept in separate bedrooms."

"So I understand. Alma?"

"No, I didn't hear anything." Her voice was little more than a whisper. Derek could see that this line of questioning upset her.

"That's something I don't quite get," he said, tapping his notebook as if he'd just discovered the inconsistency there. "Neither did the video system – see Mr. Geist leave the suite again, I mean. If you wheeled him back there at 12:40 or so, when and how did he get out of the suite later that night?"

"I have no idea," Mrs. Geist said. "That's what we hired *you* to find out, isn't it?"

"How about you, Alma – any idea?"

"Of course she doesn't have any idea!" Ida exploded. "I thought I made it clear I didn't want you torturing my granddaughter about this!"

"Asking her if she knows how her grandfather got out of the cabin without being seen by the video cameras is hardly torture, Mrs. Geist."

"Maybe not to you, Mr. DiLaurain. But Alma has been through a lot lately. And if she knew anything, she would've already told you – isn't that right, Alma?"

"Yes. I would," Alma said.

"So neither of you know anything that could possibly help with this investigation – is that what you're telling me?" Derek asked, frustration leaking into his voice.

"Absolutely nothing," Mrs. Geist said. "As we've told you from the very first."

"Well then," Derek said, closing his notebook and getting up from the sofa, "I guess I'm just wasting everyone's time. My apologies."

"You don't need to apologize, Mr. DiLaurain. Just find out what happened to my husband."

"I'm working on it, Mrs. Geist. I'm working on it."

As Derek walked back to his room, he tried to make heads or tails of the old lady's sudden protectiveness. He got the distinct feeling that she knew more than she was letting on about Alma's troubles with the law. He decided he'd need to know more as well.

*****

When Derek stepped into his suite, the first thing he saw was the blinking red light on the bedside phone. Olga was nowhere to be seen.

"Hey, I'm back!" he yelled.

"I'm in here!" his girlfriend answered from the bedroom.

She was sitting-up in bed, leaning against a half-dozen pillows as she watched a pay TV movie.

"What're you watching?" he asked, climbing up on the bed to give her a quick kiss.

"Stupid movie," she said, her eyes never moving from the big screen TV.

"Did you miss me?"

"Shh! This is good part."

He glanced at the screen and shook his head. "Hey, did someone call while I was gone?" He nodded at the blinking light.

"I did not hear. I was taking shower."

"Great," he muttered as he climbed down off the bed. "I'll be working out in the living room."

"Yes? Good."

He closed the door to the bedroom behind him as he left. His first stop was at the fridge, where he found a cool Budweiser. Then he made himself comfortable in the chair next to the phone and dialed the voicemail number.

"Derek – it's me, Danny. Hey, I found something you might find interesting. Give me a call."

He hung up and called the government whiz kid immediately.

"So what's this about something interesting?" he said the moment Danny answered.

"Don't you ever say hello?" The kid sounded harried.

"Not when the person I'm calling has something interesting to tell me."

"Maybe next time I'll tell you I have something uninteresting."

"Oh, poor baby. You want hellos? Okay – hello, hello, hello. Feel better?"

"You can be a real dick, you know that?"

"No sweet-talking me. Just the facts." His *Dragnet* impression was rusty, but serviceable.

Danny sighed audibly. "All right. So I've been trolling blogs and websites looking for anything by or about the Geists. Not surprisingly, I suppose, I found a crapload about their company, some photos at charity functions, a couple of Facebook pages…"

"Who?" Unless it was the younger generation, they didn't seem to fit the profile.

"Two of the grandkids…" Danny began, but Derek cut him off.

"But none of the oldies?"

"Nah. No social media by anyone over 30."

"So what was so interesting? Something on one of the Facebook sites?"

"Uh uh. One of the really cool things about this software is that it not only trolls for mentions and pics, but it can cross-reference and track comments between seemingly unrelated sites."

"In English?"

"The software can identify sites created by the same person or persons by shared posts or pics, even if the sites are anonymous."

The PI still didn't see what all the hoopla was about, but he played along. "Ok... And?"

"And... I came across an anonymous blog that I identified as almost certainly posted by Alma Geist. She's the granddaughter, right?"

"She is. What was so interesting about it?" Sometimes it was like pulling teeth, getting info out of Danny.

"It was posted on the day of Mr. Geist's disappearance."

"WHAT DID IT SAY?!"

"All right, all right. Keep your shirt on. It said: 'He's finally gone. I hope he burns in hell.'"

"Woa. That's pretty heavy."

"I thought you said she was the old man's favorite."

"So I was led to believe. But it doesn't look like it went both ways."

"I guess not."

Derek's mind raced. "Danny, can you tell when the blog was posted?"

"I told you, the day old man Geist disappeared."

"I know, I know. But what time?"

"Oh. Hang on a second." Derek could hear the little nerd entering keystrokes. It sounded like a chipmunk's machinegun. "One-thirty a.m." he said after a few moments.

"One-thirty? Are you sure?"

"That's what it says here. Why?"

"Because Geist was still alive at 12:40. We've got him on video."

"So?"

"So if the granddaughter was writing about him burning in hell less than an hour later, it raises the question of how she knew about it so quickly, and why she hasn't mentioned it."

"Looks like you need to talk to her again."

"Not tonight – I think they'd have me drawn and quartered if I showed up there again today. But first thing tomorrow."

"Well, good luck. Want me to check on anything else?"

"Nothing in particular. But give me a call if you turn up anything else online – by *any* of them."

"Will do."

"All right. Thanks again, Danny. You're a miracle worker."

"No problem-o. Take care of yourself."

By the time Derek hung up the phone, he was more confused than ever. How could Alma have known her grandfather was already dead by 1:30, when she'd just returned him to his cabin less than an hour earlier? And how did Geist get out of the cabin unnoticed in that brief 50 minute period?

He felt a headache coming on.

CHAPTER 12

The morning sun illuminated a brilliant blue sky and gentle rolling waves on the turquoise sea behind the resort. Derek rolled over to see if Olga was already awake and was surprised to find her side of the bed empty.

"Olga! What are you up to?!" he called out.

No response.

His girlfriend wasn't a morning person as a rule, so the PI pulled on his clothes and went out to investigate. He didn't have to go far. He found her poolside, chatting with the pool bartender.

"Good morning!" he announced as he strolled over to where the two talked.

"Well, well, well," the bartender said. "Look who's back."

Derek wasn't all that thrilled to see Olga talking with the snide little twerp to begin with, but he was most definitely in no mood to take any of his crap.

"Go shake a martini, or whatever it is you do. I was talking to my girlfriend," he snapped.

"Derek! So mean!" Olga said.

"That's okay. I'm BIG enough to take it," the bartender said with a smirk.

"Oh, I get it. Pretty witty. Or at least half-witty…"

"Listen, short-stuff," the bartender began, but Olga cut him off.

"Enough! You, go work!" she directed the bartender. "You, come!"

She swam across the pool to where she had a towel draped over her lounge chair. Derek gave the young employee the stink eye before he went to join her and got the same in return.

"Why you always start fight?" Olga asked as soon as Derek waddled to her side.

"Me?! I didn't start that."

"You never start."

"He's a jerk. Why are you always talking to him, anyway?"

"Who else I talk to? You never here."

"I'm working, you know that! As soon as I get this wrapped up, we'll have a real vacation."

"When? When wrapped up?"

"I don't know. A day or two. Hard to say."

"I not staying in room, watch movie all day. I want to feel sun!"

Her honest frustration broke the PI's foul mood. "I know, I know, honey. And I'm sorry. I didn't plan to get involved in anything like this. It just happened. We'll have plenty of time together as soon as it's ended."

"You know who kill old man?"

"Not yet. But I think I'm getting closer." He didn't add that closer didn't mean close.

She looked at him as if her intuition was ringing alarm bells. But she overrode her concerns.

"I don't like vacation without you."

"I know, sweet thing. Neither do I." He stretched on tiptoes and kissed her.

"You stay with me now?"

He wanted to get going, to talk to Alma and find out what was what with the blog. But he understood his girlfriend well enough to know he needed to hang around a while.

"Yeh, sure. Let's order some breakfast. Have you eaten?"

It turned out she hadn't, and so they spent some quality time together gnoshing-down on pancakes and eggs and bacon and multiple cups of coffee. But all the while Derek felt the clock ticking in the back of his head. As soon as it was feasible, he bowed-out.

"That was fantastic!" he said, wiping his mouth and climbing down off the chair before she could complain. "I've just got to run down some leads, and I'll be right back. We can have lunch…"

She smiled at him, shaking her head in exasperation. "You come back when you come back. I know. But now I not sad."

"That's great!" he said, giving her a quick peck on the lips, tasting the strawberry jam from her toast. "If you're happy, I'm happy!"

"Go, go!" she said, shooing him away playfully.

'I gotta be crazy, staying involved with this Geist mess,' he mused as he hurried off to interview Alma. *'Must be some kind of mental illness.'*

*****

By the time he knocked on the door to the suite, it was after 11. Later than he'd planned, but still – where did they have to go, really?

He waited, listening to footsteps approaching from inside the room. But it was Ida herself who came to the door, not her granddaughter.

"Mr. DiLaurain," she said, her expression anything but welcoming. "I thought our little conversation last night would have been enough for a day or two."

"I've come into some new information," he said. "I need to follow-up."

If anything, her countenance darkened further. "And what is this 'new information'?"

"Actually, I need to talk to your granddaughter."

"Ada? I thought I made it clear I didn't want you bothering her anymore."

"This may be important. Is she here?"

"Do you understand that you work for me?" she asked, her face a stern mask.

"I do. But I can only do my job if I'm allowed to follow the leads, no matter where they point."

"To Alma? That's ridiculous."

"Is it? Then why not let me talk to her to clear the air. Then I can do what I have to do and she can go about her business."

She stared, hard. "I'm sorry, Mr. DiLaurain, but if that's going to be your attitude, I think it best if we end your contract right here and now."

"You're firing me?"

"If you want to put it that way."

"Mrs. Geist, I think I'm getting very close to figuring out what happened to your husband…"

She held up her hand. "Stop! If your calculations include my granddaughter, I'm not interested."

Derek considered arguing further, but the look on her face persuaded him he'd be wasting his breath. "Yeh. Okay, it's your money."

"Yes, it is."

There was nothing more to say.

"I'll have them send your last check to the address we have on file," she said. "Thank you for your work."

With that, she closed the door.

'Something's not right here,' the PI mused as he walked away. *'And if she thinks I'm giving up now, she's got another thing coming.'*

*****

The desk clerk looked studiously bored, barely managing to lift his eyelids to watch Derek cross to where he sat behind a polished dark wood counter.

"May I help you?" he asked. He showed no sign he was interested in doing so.

"I was supposed to meet another of your guests here this morning – Alma Geist? But I'm running a little late. Have you seen her by any chance? About five foot seven, reddish-brown hair…"

"I know what Ms. Geist looks like," he snapped.

"Good. Then, did you see her this morning?"

"She left about a half-hour ago."

"Did she happen to mention where she was going?"

The clerk eyed him suspiciously. "I thought you were supposed to go with her."

"We hadn't decided where we were going."

"Oh? Well, she didn't say anything to me." He made it very clear that Derek was not a priority.

The PI nodded while at the same time digging into his pocket. He pulled out a twenty dollar bill and folded it twice.

"Did you, by any chance, overhear her talking with the cab driver?" he asked, slipping the twenty across the counter.

The clerk's eyes dipped to the bill for just an instant, before his hand reached out and grabbed it like it was too hot to touch.

"She might have mentioned that she wanted to go to Horseshoe Bay," he said, turning to flip through some paperwork.

"Thanks, for *all* your help," the PI sneered, but the put-down didn't even register with the clerk. Derek was about to launch into a less subtle attack when a customer came in through the front doors. He decided to let sleepy clerks lie.

Remmy was at the entrance to the resort five minutes after Derek called.

"Where to, Boss-man?" the cabbie asked as the PI came toward his taxi. He was wearing a bright pink golf shirt, bright red Bermuda shorts, and a baseball cap with both ear flaps and a neck covering.

"Horseshoe Bay – how long?"

"Ten, fifteen minutes. Everything is ten to fifteen minutes in Bermuda."

"All right then, let's go."

True to his word, Remmy turned down the short roadway to the iconic beach just 12 minutes later. But from the small parking lot adjacent to a decidedly low-key snack bar, it didn't look like much at all.

"*This* is Horseshoe Bay?" the PI asked.

"Don't get your shorts in a knot, Boss-man," the cabbie said. "Like most of Bermuda, there's more here than first meets the eye."

Unconvinced, Derek nonetheless climbed out of the van and made his way along a worn sand pathway toward the beach. Not thirty yards ahead, the reality of the Bay became crystal clear – as clear as the gorgeous blue-green water lapping against a long crescent of the pinkish sand the island was so famous for.

But as he scanned the near-deserted beach, Alma was nowhere to be found.

"Damn it!" he muttered.

"Can't see the young lady?" a familiar voice asked from close behind.

He glanced over his shoulder to see Remmy looking past him to the beach beyond.

"She's not here."

"Maybe, maybe not."

The PI turned to face his driver. "And what exactly does that mean?" That's all he needed, a Kung-fu philosopher cabbie.

"It means that the lady miiiight just be taking advantage of the privacy afforded by the other beaches."

"What other beaches?" He hated guessing games.

"There are several little pocket beaches there, at the far end of Horseshoe." He nodded toward the rocks that came down to the sea. "Maybe she's at one of them."

"Can you show me?"

"Sure Boss-man, anything you say." The cabbie smiled broadly.

The two of them walked along the pristine beach, past the half-dozen or so hearty sunbathers, and up to a small sandy track just to the left and above the rocks that marked the end of the bay. The track paralleled the beachline and gave them a bird's-eye view of the numerous mini-beaches that dotted the coast over the next half mile or so. They'd only walked for a few minutes, past the two closest beaches, when they identified a familiar form on the third. Alma was stretched out on a beach towel, a bottle of wine and an empty glass resting next to a small backpack.

"How the hell do I get down there?" he asked his guide.

"No problem, Boss," Remmy said, leading him to a gulley carved into the stone by run-off. It wasn't fancy, but it'd serve.

"Watch your step," Remmy warned. "Lots of loose rock."

Derek nodded his thanks and made his way carefully down the gulley to the beach. The sound of the lapping waves covered his climb; the young woman showed no sign she was aware of his approach.

So it was little surprise that she jumped up when Derek identified himself. "Well, look who we have here! What a coincidence," he said, his attempt at convincing her barely pro-forma.

"Mr. DiLaurain! What are you doing here?!"

"Just out for a walk on the beach," he lied. "You?"

"I… I just wanted to get away from all that," she motioned with her hand. "You know." She slurred her words ever so slightly.

"Must be quite distressing, losing your grandfather and all."

"Yes. It was."

"What do you have there?" he asked, indicating the wine bottle. "Chardonnay?"

She glanced at the bottle quickly, and then back at the PI. Was that a guilty look he saw?

"It's a DuMol," she announced, as if that explained everything.

"Oh? How wonderful." In fact, Derek had no idea on earth what a DuMol was, but if she thought it was worth mentioning, it must be good.

"Would you like some?" she asked, but without much conviction.

"Oh no, thank you. I'm more a beer connoisseur myself."

"Oh? That's right; I remember now."

There was a moment of awkward silence, one of those times when both parties know there's something that needs to be said, but neither is quite prepared to be the first to bring it up. Derek was the first – sort of.

"Beautiful beach," he hedged.

"Yes, isn't it remarkable that you can find such a lovely beach, with so few people, on a tourist island like this."

"It is, yes."

She looked out at the water, as if hoping he'd take the hint and leave her to her privacy. He couldn't do that.

"I was wondering…" he began.

She turned abruptly, every sense alert to his overture.

"Yes?"

Wide-eyed, shoulders tense, he could almost see her lower lip quiver.

"When did you start writing your blog?"

He watched her closely. There was no denying he'd hit close to home.

"Blog? What blog?"

Her voice was pitched a half-octave too high, on the verge of cracking.

"The blog you run under the title 'Thoughts From the Edge'. That's yours, isn't it?"

She stared at him, struck dumb.

"I... Why do you say that?"

He needed to step delicately. He sensed that he had her on the ropes, but one wrong move could send her running.

"The Internet is a wonderful thing," he said, now looking out to sea as if she were merely a secondary interest, "but it's nowhere near as anonymous as we all seem to think. Everything that's put out there – photos, websites, *blogs* – they all leave a trail. Electronic tracks, if you will."

"Oh?"

"Oh yeh. And if you know enough about the Internet – or know someone who does – you can track nearly anything that's been posted back to the person who originated it."

"I... I didn't know that."

"Not too many people do. Of course, most of the time, no one bothers to track all the garbage that ends up on the 'Net, but every now and then, someone does."

"What does all this have to do with me?" she asked, her voice ever more brittle.

"I have a blog posting here," he said, searching around in his pockets for the paper he'd printed out. "Ah, here we are. It says, 'He's finally gone. I hope he burns in hell.' Sound familiar?"

Alma stared into empty space. "Should it?" she muttered.

"Thing is, it was posted less than an hour after we think your grandfather went overboard. Before anyone actually knew that he *had* gone overboard. Quite the coincidence, don't you think?"

"It... it's not about him," she said after a short pause.

"It isn't? Who then? Who is it about?"

"A guy. An... ex-boyfriend."

"Ah. So it *was* just a coincidence that it appeared at almost the exact time your grandfather was going over the side?"

"Must be." She regained a hint of composure. "Just a coincidence."

Derek nodded to himself. He folded the note and slid it back into his pocket. "I see. You didn't by any chance see your grandfather later that night, after you brought him back from your walk up on deck, I mean?"

"I already told you I didn't." He could tell by the strength returning to her voice that his moment had passed. She'd survived his sneak attack.

"Yes, I guess you did, didn't you. Well, I'll leave you to your wine. Still have a lot to check out."

He started to go.

"I thought Grandma fired you," she called after him.

He stopped and turned back to face her. "She did. Now I'm doing it on my own. I don't like unfinished cases. Bad for the reputation."

He smiled, nodded once, and began the long slog back up the rocky hillside to where Remmy waited.

"Any luck?" the cabbie asked as soon as Derek reappeared.

"Don't know yet," he said, his gaze locked on the young woman sunbathing just below them. "Sometimes it takes a while for a seed to sprout, you know?"

Remmy nodded.

CHAPTER 13

Before he tracked down Olga to tell her he was back at the Coral Queen, before he even made a needed stop at the bathroom, Derek called a familiar number in northern Virginia.

"Brady, it's me, Derek."

"Hey, how's it going with that investigation? I spoke to Danny…"

"I think we're almost there," he said.

"Gut feeling, or has something come up?"

"A little of both. Something's going on with the granddaughter – Alma. Can't quite pin it down yet, but soon. Although I won't be getting much help from the Geist crew."

"How do you mean?"

"The old lady fired me. Said I was *harassing* the granddaughter."

"Were you?"

"That's what I like – can always depend on you to back me up."

"I got your back, but I know you all too well."

"I asked her a few questions, that's all."

"Right. Anything I can do?"

"If you talk to Chez, ask him if the court ordered a psychological profile for Alma back when she got popped as a teen. With three arrests so close together, I'd imagine they'd want to know what caused the transformation from good girl to hooker."

"You know, of course, that those profiles – especially for a teen – would be sealed?"

"That's why I'm asking Chez. Who can get around irritating regs better than a cop?"

"Regs? I think those are called *laws*."

"You say tomatoes…"

"I say you're a raving lunatic."

"Ooo, talk dirty to me. I'm getting hot just thinking about it."

"I think someone besides Alma needs a psychological profile."

"Now now, let's not get nasty. How's everything going back there?"

"Not bad. RG3 looks like he may be coming around…"

"Wow. Now who needs a psych profile?"

"Optimism is not a mental disease."

"Supporting the 'Skins may be. But we can discuss that further when I get home. For now, I'm off to see

the local police inspector who's been assigned this case.
I've got a few questions for him."

"Say hi to Olga."

"Same on your end."

As Derek hung up, he ran through all the evidence
piece by piece. He never discounted his hunches, and he
was getting a major league hunch that Alma knew more
than she was letting-on. Maybe Chief Inspector Trott
could help him figure out where she fit into this whole
mess. But not until he'd taken a long-overdue whizz...

*****

Trott was right where Derek had last seen him:
behind the cluttered desk in his downtown office.

"Mr. DiLaurain!" the Inspector said when the
diminutive PI strolled into the office. "What brings you
down here?"

"I was in the area," he lied, "and was wondering if
you'd gotten anything back from the lab – on the DNA
evidence?"

"As a matter of fact, I think we got something a
short while ago," he said as he sifted through the piles
of paper on his desk. "I haven't even had time to look at
it myself." He eventually located the paper and held it
up for a quick read. "Here we go..."

"So? Anything of interest?"

"As a matter of fact…"

"Yes?"

"They matched the DNA under Mr. Geist's fingernails."

"With who?"

"Well, to begin with, with himself."

"He scratched *himself*? Did the coroner find any scratches that would suggest they'd been self-inflicted?" People didn't normally scratch themselves hard enough to draw blood. And from what he'd seen when they'd visited the morgue, he'd had a good deal of skin *and* blood under the nails of *both* hands. That would have left one hell of a scratch.

The Inspector shook his head as if sorting out the implications. "It *is* very strange…"

"Were there other matches?"

"It's not clear. At least not to me. Seems there was a mix of DNA…"

"Can we talk to someone who can sort it out?"

"Of course! We don't have many DNA specialists here on the island, but I have a contact in Boston…"

"Can we call him?"

"Now?"

"Unless there's some reason why we can't."

"No, no. Sure, let me get his number."

The Inspector dug into his cellphone contact list and found the number. Dr. Peter Jenkinson was not only a professor at MIT, but ran his own lab inside the 128 Beltway. The Inspector warned Derek that Jenkinson would probably be unavailable, since he was an expert witness in much demand as well as a full professor. To his surprise, the professor was in his office and answered himself.

Trott explained the situation briefly and Jenkinson asked him to fax the results he'd obtained from the earlier DNA test. In minutes, he called them back.

"Okay, got the results," he said over the speakerphone in Trott's office. "From what I see here, you've got one of two possibilities: either your victim scratched both himself and someone unknown quite deeply, at virtually the exact same time – not very likely, in my opinion, or the person he scratched was just one or two generations removed from the victim."

"Excuse me Prof," Derek interrupted, "but just to be clear, are you saying the person he scratched was a family member?"

"Exactly. A direct descendant – son or daughter, perhaps grandchild."

"How definite is that analysis?"

"Over 99%. The genetic similarities are too great to be chance. It's a family member – I'd bet on it."

After a little more back and forth the Inspector thanked Jenkinson and hung up the phone.

"So? What do you make of that?" he asked.

"I'm not sure. Can you get a DNA sample from all the Geist kids and grandkids?"

"I don't know. Are they all still here on the island?"

"I doubt it. I think some of them went on with the cruise. But how about the ones still here?"

"Shouldn't be a problem. I think I can get a court order to take swab samples."

"What if they refuse?"

"Unless they get a judge to stay the testing, they have no choice."

"They've got the money to hire the best lawyers you've got over here."

"Let's not get ahead of ourselves. The testing isn't all that intrusive – a quick swab with a q-tip inside the mouth. I don't see why they'd object."

"You don't know the Geists," Derek said.

"Well, let's find out." Trott picked up his phone, punched in a number and waited. "Judge Biggins, please," he said after a few moments. "Judge, Chief Inspector Trott here. How're you doing this fine day? Good, good. Hey Judge, I've got a situation here." Within minutes he had his authority.

"No problem on that end," he said as he hung up.

"Do you have the personnel to get it done quickly?"

He smiled, held up one finger and dialed once again. "Jenny, can we get a DNA evidence team out to…" He turned to Derek. "Was it the Coral Queen?"

"And Aaron at the Hibiscus."

"…the Coral Queen and the Hibiscus to get some swabs from the Geist family members staying at each resort?" He nodded as he heard the reply. "Good. Tell them it's time-sensitive, so get their butts out there – today." He laughed at the answer and hung up. "They're on their way, almost," he told Derek. "If they can track the Geists down, we can have their swabs on an evening flight to Boston, and can get the results no later than the day after tomorrow."

"Excellent! I owe you, Inspector."

"Solve the case, and your debt's paid," Trott joked.

"We'll see what we can do."

As Derek left police headquarters, he glanced back up toward Church Street and saw the sturdy stone spires of a big Anglican Church just a couple of blocks away. With all the vagaries of the Geist case still outstanding, he seriously considered whether prayer should be his next move.

*****

When he opened the door to his suite at the Coral Queen, Derek didn't know whether he'd find a happy Olga, an unhappy Olga, or no Olga at all. It turned out she was still engrossed in an old movie and had hardly noticed his absence. He wasn't sure whether he liked that or not.

"You are back?" she asked, barely looking up from her TV.

"I am. Got some interesting info from the Chief Inspector."

"How nice."

"The DNA test on old man Geist was very revealing."

"I'm sure."

The PI debated whether to break her concentration with a tirade about her blatant lack of interest in his investigation, but decided to let viewing Russians lie. Or something like that.

"I'll be back," he said.

"That is good," she said.

He grabbed an orange from the welcome plate the resort had provided upon their arrival and opened his laptop to take a quick look to see if he'd received any new emails: a couple of junk ads, a reminder to pay his utility bill, and a new message from Danny. He opened the last.

'Derek: just came upon these. Used facial recognition software to scour the Net for any pics your Alma might have posted. Don't know if any of these will prove useful, but wanted you to see them.' He'd provided a link to a cloud storage site.

When the PI clicked the link he saw that Danny had uploaded 22 photos. He set about opening them one by one. As he might've expected, there were photos of Alma with friends, at the beach, at various parties or dinners, at somebody's birthday, in front of landmarks, and… a photo of the young woman when she was maybe 21 or so, wearing a black leather jacket while riding a 600cc Suzuki motorcycle. She wasn't a passenger, but sat all alone looking entirely comfortable on the big ol' bike. The second he saw her, a memory of the shooter the day before flashed through his mind. Could it be?

He ran a search of motorcycle rental companies on the Island and followed-up with phone calls to each of them. He told them that his niece had rented a bike the day before but had forgotten the name of the company. "She's a little bit of an airhead," he prompted. "She lost one of her riding gloves: have you seen it?" It only took three calls before he found the people who'd rented the bike. At that point he carried the laptop to the reception desk and persuaded the bored clerk – with a five dollar bill – to print out the photo.

"Cute girl," he said as he handed the print to Derek.

"Yeh, a real killer," the PI said.

He dumped the laptop back in his room and made his way straight to the Geist suite. Several knocks on the door and rings of the buzzer produced no response. But now that he'd had his first real sniff of a scent on the case, he wasn't going to be dissuaded so easily. He walked around the bungalow to the private pool ringed by shrubbery just behind it. He peeked through the flowering greenery and discovered Mrs. Geist stretched out on a lounge chair, wearing a white beach robe, engrossed in a hardback book. Using his size to good advantage, he slipped through a small gap in the hedge and walked stealthily over to where she sat.

She was so involved in the book she didn't notice his approach until he cleared his throat loudly no more than five or six feet from where she sat reading.

"Oh!" she said with a flinch, "you startled me, Mr. DiLaurain."

"Sorry about that. Anything good?" he asked, nodding toward the novel.

"Oh, just some mystery. Good to keep my mind off everything else." She looked at him, and then back to the closed sliding glass door at the rear of the bungalow. "How did you get in here?"

"The door was unlocked," he said.

"Oh? I'll have to see about that." A moment of awkward silence. "Did you want to talk to me about something?"

"I did. I've just come back from having a conversation with Chief Inspector Trott in Hamilton," he said, boosting himself up onto the lounger next to her. "About the results of the DNA test on the blood and skin found under your husband's fingernails."

"I thought I made it clear that you were no longer working on that investigation," she growled, closing the book and laying it down next to her.

"No longer working for *you*. When I take-on a case, I like to see it through to its conclusion."

"How diligent of you." Her tone was anything but complimentary.

"One of my associates back in the States came across some photos on the Internet that I found interesting." He opened the envelope.

"Isn't that nice."

"There's one in particular I wanted to show you." He took the photo of Alma on the motorcycle and handed it to the old woman.

She smiled. "Oh yes. Alma was quite the speed demon there for a while."

"Did you know she took a ride yesterday?" He watched closely for a reaction.

Ida barely blinked. "Oh? Did she? I didn't realize she was still riding. But then again, I believe the only way to see this island on your own is by renting a bike – no car rentals, you know."

"Does she own a black leather jacket?"

Mrs. Geist's eyes narrowed to slits. "Why do you want to know?"

"Just a theory I'm working on."

"About my husband's death?"

"Might have something to do with it."

"I don't think I want to continue this conversation, Mr. DiLaurain. And before you *drop* by again, please call."

"If it's not me asking these questions, it'll be the police. I'm compelled to surrender any information I turn up."

"Somehow I doubt that. And furthermore, I very much doubt the Chief Inspector will share your predilection for harassing my granddaughter. Good afternoon." She turned back to her novel.

"You know, Mrs. Geist, if I didn't know any better, I'd think you weren't overly eager to find your husband's killer."

She didn't bother to glance up.

"Good day, Mr. DiLaurain."

He was tempted to follow-up one more time, but on second thought decided he'd stirred the pot enough. Now he just had to sit back and see what boiled up.

*****

"Got the psych profile you were asking about," Detective Chesley said as soon as Derek answered the phone.

"Good man. Anything interesting?"

"Actually, the most interesting part was what *wasn't* there."

"How do you mean?"

"I mean there's a section that talks about suspected abuse, but most of that report is missing."

"Abuse? What kind?"

"Not described."

"And I suppose there's nothing about the perp?"

"You know, you should be a PI or something. You've got a talent for the obvious."

"Then I guess I should've been a cop."

Chez ignored him. "I'm guessing the missing section was where she talked about whoever did it to her."

"More than likely. I don't suppose you can track down the shrink she talked to...?"

"And what? Admit that I illegally accessed a sealed evaluation? I don't think so."

"Yeh. Not a good idea. Well then, I guess we'll have to find another way to get that name."

"Maybe her old man was beating on her?"

"You mean her father, or a boyfriend?"

"I don't know. Could be either."

"Maybe, but it doesn't smell right."

"You have any other ideas?"

"I'm already working on it. Even though I didn't know until just now that that's what I was looking for."

"Wanna explain?"

"Not quite yet. But if my hunch is right, I should have something fairly soon. Within a day or two."

"And if you're wrong?"

"Chez! Don't you remember? I've got a talent for this crap."

"Oh yeh. It's all coming back to me."

"Thanks for the eval. Might've been the missing piece in this crazy puzzle."

"I live to serve."

Derek nodded to himself as he hung up the phone. It was getting interesting-er and interesting-er.

*****

Derek felt like he was closing in on… something. But he had two issues to deal with: the motive and the timing. He'd seen Alma wheel the old man back to his suite at 12:40. How the hell did he die an hour later without ever getting out of the suite? And if the granddaughter had something to do with it, why? He decided to review the tapes one last time and called Ms. Earthal. He found her onboard the Princess at its next port in the Bahamas.

"Mr. DiLaurain! I must admit, I'm surprised to hear from you."

"Why's that?"

"I heard from one of Mrs. Geist's people that you were no longer working that investigation."

"Don't believe everything you read. I'm not working for *her*, but I don't give up on an investigation until it's finished."

"Admirable. What can I do for you?"

He explained that he needed to review the security tapes one more time and asked if they could be sent to him.

"I don't see why not, since you've already reviewed them. You will have to sign a non-disclosure agreement, of course. I don't want to see any of our tapes on TV or the Internet."

"Done."

"I'll fax it to you right now. Then I'll ask Todd or Eric to upload the tapes to one of the cloud services. You can download them from there?"

"I might need a little coaching but yeh, I think I can handle it."

He gave her the resort's fax number and hung up.

"You look like you thinking hard," Olga said, strolling into the suite's living room.

"Still trying to figure out the Geist case. The parts don't add up."

"Add up?"

"Old man Geist died with sleeping pills in his bloodstream and water in his lungs, but I saw him talking to Alma less than an hour before he died up on the upper deck. And he never left his suite after he returned. Makes no sense."

"Old Russian saying: if thing not as it seems, must be something else."

"Was Sherlock Holmes Russian?"

She looked at him with a questioning glance.

"Never mind," he said. "I gotta go get a fax that should be waiting for me at the front desk, and then I'll be reviewing some video tapes."

"Anything good?" She bobbed her eyebrows suggestively.

"Oh yeh, hot stuff. An old fart being wheeled along hallways on the boat. It's got Oscar written all over it."

"Who Oscar?"

He reached up and pulled her down by the arm to a height where he could kiss her on the forehead.

"See you in a little while. I need to run down to reception."

"You always say 'little while'." She was pouting.

"Warm the sheets up for me."

"Sheets already warm."

"Then keep them that way."

He knew better than to continue the conversation; he couldn't win. So he kissed her again and headed to the reception area.

This time the clerk recognized him.

"What can I do for you, Mr. DiLaurain?"

"Did a fax just arrive for me?"

"Not that I've seen. Let me take a look." He was back in seconds with the agreement.

"Are you working on some sort of book or movie?" he asked, surveying the paper as he prepared to hand it over.

"You're paid to deliver the fax, not read it," the PI complained, snatching the page from his hand.

"Oh, I'm terribly sorry, Mr. DiLaurain. I didn't mean anything…"

Derek handed the flustered clerk a twenty dollar bill. "You didn't see this fax and I wasn't here to get it. Understand?"

The clerk looked first at the twenty, and then at Derek. "Haven't seen you all day."

"Good man."

He quickly signed the document and gave it back to the clerk. "Here's the number I want you to send it to. Again, you didn't send it, and I wasn't here."

The clerk smiled. "No fax. No you. Got it."

Ten minutes later, the PI slipped quietly back into his suite and began downloading the security camera footage from the site Ms. Earthal had emailed to him.

As the laptop rang out its familiar opening notes, Olga stuck her head into the big room.

"You back fast."

"Told you. Now, I've gotta review this stuff for a while, so you go on and watch your movies."

"Sheets are warm…"

"When I get there they'll be hot."

Olga's smile said it all.

It took more than twenty minutes to download all the footage, even compressed as it was. Derek opened a beer and checked the program guide on the living room TV to see if there were any sports shows he could watch while he waited, until finally, the entire file was downloaded.

Sipping his beer as he reviewed the footage, he kicked off his sneakers and leaned back in a comfy easy chair, punching buttons on the video software player to fast-forward, reverse and pause the footage whenever he thought something was worth a second look. But despite his best efforts, nothing jumped out at him. His patience was already wearing thin by the time Olga came out to see what progress he was making.

"You find something?" she asked, coming behind him to look over his shoulder at the computer screen.

"Yeh – that a cruise ship is a pretty damn boring place to be late at night," he grumbled.

Olga watched along with him as he re-played the sequence when Alma wheeled her grandfather out of the suite, then up on deck for a breath of fresh air before returning to the suite at 12:40. The time was burned into the video in the top left-hand corner.

"Mr. Geist look pretty out of it," she said as the wheelchair emerged from the suite. In fact, Derek had thought the same thing. "He'd probably already taken his sleeping pills," he said. "More than likely half-asleep."

"Ah." They watched for another few seconds. Alma pushed the wheelchair along the hallway until they arrived at the elevator, which they took up to the top deck. Derek rewound the video and noted the timecode just as the elevator closed, and then when it opened again up on deck. The Princess security team had done a good job editing the various camera angles together into one continuous scene. Of course they'd also sent the raw footage, but for the moment he was concentrating on the movement of the wheelchair.

From the elevator they turned to the left and passed directly behind the ship's huge smokestack. Moments later, in what amounted to a jump cut, they reappeared at the other side of the stack and paused beside a railing to look out at the dark sea below.

"Look strange," Olga said.

"Yeh, they cut out the footage of when they were behind the stack. Apparently they don't have any cameras back there. Too expensive to cover every inch of the boat."

He rewound the video and noted the time code when they disappeared behind the stack, and then again when they reappeared. "Fifty-seven seconds," he said.

"What?"

"They were behind the stack for fifty-seven seconds."

"So?"

"It's not very far. Does it seem like a long time to you?"

"Maybe deck there is not clear."

"What, like ropes, or equipment or something?"

"Could be."

"I'll have to check." He wrote himself another note.

They watched silently as Geist and his granddaughter stood at the railing and looked out at the sky and sea.

"What they look for?" Olga asked.

"Just looking – at the ocean, the stars, whatever."

The old man sat there for twenty-three minutes and seven seconds before he seemed to nod-off in his chair. Alma leaned down and said something into his ear, and when he didn't react she released the brake on the wheelchair and took him back along the same route. This time Derek jotted down the time code on each end of the detour behind the smokestack.

"Twelve minutes and four seconds," he announced when they reappeared.

"Very much time."

"Over eleven minutes more," the PI confirmed. "Why?"

"Stop to watch… fish?"

"Could be."

The elevator trip down took almost exactly the same amount of time as the trip up. Then they came straight back to the suite. Alma stopped in the hallway, took out a keycard, opened the door, and started to wheel him inside.

"Nice bracelet," Olga said, apropos to nothing.

"What?" He didn't want to sound annoyed, but non sequiturs always pushed his buttons.

"He wear nice bracelet."

Derek didn't say a word, but rewound the video to the moment before the wheelchair disappeared back into the Geist suite. He put it into slow-mo and leaned forward to get a better look. Sure enough, just as Alma was trying to maneuver the wheelchair through the narrow cabin door, Mr. Geist stirred and reached out to help brace the door so they could get through.

And there, on *his* wrist, was what appeared to be a large, very unique turquoise bracelet. The image wasn't as clear as he might hope, but there was no doubt in his mind what he was looking at: Derek was pretty certain he'd seen that particular bracelet before. He jumped up and kissed Olga full on the lips.

"You're a genius!" he shouted to his startled girlfriend.

"I am?"

"You are!" He grabbed the laptop, pulled on his sneaks and started for the door.

"Where you go?" Olga called after him.

"Be back in a few!"

The same clerk, looking as bored as ever, was sitting behind the counter when the PI arrived at the reception desk minutes later.

"I need you to print something for me," he said without introduction.

"Of course, Mr. DiLaurain!" the clerk said, pulling himself to attention with obvious effort.

"Can we connect this laptop to your printer?"

"I don't see why not."

Derek played the video again, pausing on the frame where the bracelet was most clearly visible. Then he hit 'Print Screen' and captured the image.

"Okay, this is what I want you to print." He handed him the laptop.

"This?" the clerk asked, looking askance at the somewhat blurry image.

"That's it. Do you have a color printer?"

"We do."

"Then make it color, please. Two copies."

While the clerk was connecting the computer and making copies, Derek called Caroline Earthal back on the Princess. He asked her to take a few photos for him and make some measurements. She was confused, but agreed. Just seconds after he hung up, the clerk delivered the prints.

"Not exactly high-def," he said as he handed them over.

Derek took a quick look. The lighting in the hallway was less than ideal, but there was no doubt in his mind what the photo showed. He slipped the clerk another twenty.

"You know the drill," he said.

"You weren't here and you didn't ask me to do anything for you," the clerk repeated with a smile.

"Smart kid." He pointed to the laptop. "Can I leave that here for a little while?"

"Sure, no problem."

"Thanks. And no one touches it, right?"

"I'll lock it in our safe until you come back for it."

"You're a prince."

Photos in hand, Derek went straight to Mrs. Geist's suite. This time, when he rang the doorbell Alma answered.

"Oh! I don't think Grandma wants to see you, Mr. DiLaurain."

"I bet. Tell her I've just cracked the case."

"What?"

"Tell her I think I know what happened to her husband." He stared at her without blinking. She flinched.

"I… I'll go tell her. Hold on a second." She shut the door, leaving him waiting outside.

Seconds became minutes, and still Alma didn't return. The PI was just about to go around to the other side of the bungalow again, when a most unfriendly voice called out from the walkway behind him.

"Hey, weren't you told to stay away from those people?"

Derek turned to see two men, one the size of a small mountain, the other not quite so large but still considerably bigger than Derek, striding toward him with scowls on their faces that would've frozen a daiquiri.

"What's it to you?"

"Mrs. Geist has asked that you be escorted from the property," the smaller of the two said as both men crowded-in menacingly close to the PI. To Derek it felt as if he were standing between two high-rises.

"I'm a guest here," he said, knowing full well it wouldn't sway the two security men.

"Not anymore."

The bigger of the two grabbed him by the arm. "Let's go."

Derek shook his arm free. "I don't need your help." When he turned to leave the smaller man stopped him with a hand to his shoulder.

"You need to go back to your room. We'll wait while you pack."

Derek fumed, helpless. Geist had all the money in the world. These people weren't going to listen to him. "This won't look good in Trip Advisor," he said, taking his best shot.

The bigger guy chuckled. "Funny little twerp, aren't ya."

"Glad I entertain you."

Back at the suite, Derek had to explain to Olga why they were leaving.

"We must call police!" she shouted.

"They could come up with a dozen reasons why we were evicted. Hell, the old lady just needs to stop paying for the room. Better to pack and go."

"But…"

"We can't win this time. But it's just one battle. The war still rages," the PI explained, his eyes gleaming.

"War?"

"Just pack. I'll find us another place."

Derek called Remmy to get his recommendation where to stay.

"Don't like the Queen?" the cabbie asked.

"It doesn't like us."

"What happened? Did you…?"

"Just come get us," the PI interrupted. "I'll explain when you get here."

*****

The ride to the Water's Edge Lodge took over a half-hour.

"Where the hell is this place?!" Derek finally asked when they'd been driving for what seemed an eternity on the tiny island.

"Almost there. Stay calm," Remmy advised as he continued his 30 mph cruise through the narrow roadways to the eastern end of the island.

"I didn't think the island was big enough to drive this long."

"Not big, but long. And we don't have freeways like in the States."

"More like driveways," the PI grumbled.

Remmy laughed. "Driveways. That's good, Boss."

Derek wasn't smiling. And when they arrived at the Water's Edge, just outside of St. George, it was Olga's turn to frown.

"This is where we stay?" she asked, eyes wide with shock.

The Water's Edge was a slightly seedy hold-over from the 1950's, a pale green low-rise with a few dozen rooms stacked motel style. At first glance, it wasn't the Coral Queen. Nor at second glance.

"Who's their decorator, Andy Warhol?" Derek asked as he stared into room 107. Pale pink and yellow walls. Four inch black and white tiles in the bathroom. Worn carpeting that looked older than the building. Even an antique 21" CRT TV.

Olga looked as if she were going to cry.

"It's clean, the beds are good, and the shower works," Remmy said in self-defense. "You'll see. Good value for the money."

"We don't have much choice, at least for today," Derek said to his girlfriend. "If we don't like it, we can always move."

"Do they have pool?" Olga asked.

Derek looked to Remmy. "Of course they have a pool," the cabbie said. "Not Olympic size, but you can swim."

Derek had heard and seen enough. He was tired. Tired of the whole Geist mess. He slipped Remmy a tip and sent him on his way. Then he climbed up on the king-size bed to take a break from all the lying, manipulation and cover-ups.

As he lay there, Olga unpacking to a constant sotto voce commentary in Russian, he mentally outlined his plans for the coming day. The Geists probably thought they'd scared him off. But they didn't know Derek E. DiLaurain. If he'd ever considered giving up on the investigation – and despite his denials it *had* crossed his mind when the paychecks stopped coming – now he was pissed. He was going to find out who offed the old man if it killed him. Better yet, if it killed *them*.

*****

When Derek cracked open his eyelids the following morning, he was taken aback to find the other half of the bed empty. "God damn it!" he muttered. "Now where's she gone off to?"

He pulled on a pair of shorts and a t-shirt, slipped into his sandals, and headed out to find her. It didn't take long. As soon as he stepped out of their first floor room he saw her sunning next to the mini-pool.

"You're up early," he said when he'd made his way over to her lounge chair. He braced for another cycle of whining.

"Nice day. Sun feel good," she said, shading her eyes with one hand.

"How did you sleep?"

"Good. You?"

He hadn't thought about it much, but he had to admit, "Not bad. Pretty comfortable bed."

"Better than Coral Queen."

Again, she was right. "Looks like Remmy steered us straight."

"He steer straight?" she asked.

"He hit the nail on the head when he recommended this place."

"He hit nail?"

"Never mind. Ready for some breakfast?"

Olga was content to stay right where she was, but asked Derek to bring her back a croissant. He promised he would, then went back to their room and dressed, by which time Remmy was outside waiting for him.

"So, what d'ya think?" he asked as soon as he saw the PI.

"About the hotel? Not bad. Pretty good, really."

"What I say?"

"You da' Man," Derek said. "Now take me someplace I can get a decent breakfast without hocking my laptop."

"You got it, Boss."

Mel's was a tiny eatery just a block off the main square in St. Georges. 'Main square' was somewhat misleading: just an open space with some 18th century stocks (the kind people put their hands and head thru when they were convicted of witchcraft or some equally horrible offense back in Colonial times), the town hall, a tourist information center, and a handful of small shops. Quaint, in a way.

"Nice, huh?" Remmy asked as he walked Derek from their parking space to Mel's.

"Quaint, in a way," the PI said.

Mel's was barely big enough to turn around in, but they featured "one of the best cod breakfasts in this part of the island," or so Remmy assured Derek.

"They eat fish for breakfast?" he asked.

"It's an island. We eat a lot of fish."

Derek decided to give it a whirl and ordered the local favorite. Remmy ordered eggs and toast.

"I thought you locals like fish for breakfast," the PI said when he heard the cabbie's order.

"I said we *eat* a lot of fish, not necessarily like it."

"You should've been a lawyer. Hey, excuse me a minute. I need to make a call."

Derek stepped out into the narrow cobblestone alleyway behind the restaurant and called Chief Inspector Trott.

"Chief Inspector, Derek DiLaurain here."

"Mr. DiLaurain! Are you still on-island?"

"I am. Why do you ask?"

"We received a complaint from Mrs. Geist that you were 'stalking' her and her granddaughter, and they'd asked their bodyguards to send you on your way. Thought maybe you'd gone back to the States."

"And leave an open investigation?! Not a chance. I think we need to meet."

"Oh? More ideas about Mr. Geist's death?"

"More than just ideas. I've got something to show you."

They agreed to meet in two hours at the Inspector's office. Then Derek called Arnie to confirm a hunch. It was confirmed.

*****

"You know, old lady Geist really doesn't like you very much," Trott said when Derek had taken a seat in his office. "She's on the warpath."

"Yeh, she's made that pretty damn clear," the PI said. "But I think she's protecting someone."

The Inspector leaned forward. "Oh?"

He took out his laptop. "Like I said on the phone, I've got something I want you to take a look at."

Derek brought up the security footage from the night of Mr. Geist's death, and pointed out the green blob on Geist's wrist.

"What are we looking at?" the Inspector said, squinting to make heads or tails of the grainy image.

"It's a bracelet!" Derek explained.

"Pretty gaudy for an old guy like Geist," Trott said.

"But not so gaudy for his wife."

"What?! Are you telling me that's not Mr. Geist in the wheelchair?"

"Let's just say that Mrs. Geist has a bracelet that looks *exactly* like what you just saw in the video. I've seen it myself."

"But… that doesn't make any sense! We haven't heard anything about the Geists having marital problems."

"I'm not saying they did. As a matter of fact, I have a very different take on all this."

"Oh. Are you going to share?"

For the next hour the PI outlined his theory and worked with the Chief Inspector to develop a plan to reveal exactly what happened to Arnold Geist Sr. Derek asked Trott to make some official inquiries for him and the Inspector agreed – with a proviso.

"You realize what will happen if it turns out you're wrong, right?" Trott asked the PI when they'd finished.

"Hell hath no fury like a rich woman who doesn't get her way."

"I'll be pounding a beat in Pembroke and you'll be lucky if you still have a license."

"There's something there, Inspector, I can feel it. We just need to prove I'm right."

Trott shook his head as if doubting his own sanity. "All right, I'll back you up. But don't let me down."

"I'll do my best."

He only hoped that would be good enough.

CHAPTER 14

Being small had advantages, and disadvantages. On the one hand, Derek could get into places and hide behind objects that full-size people couldn't. On the other, if anyone did see him it was unlikely they'd mistake him for someone else. No false mustache or wig would disguise the fact that he was three-foot-five, on tiptoes.

So when Remmy drove him back to the Coral Queen, the cabbie didn't pull into the main entrance and drop him at the reception area. Instead, he snaked his way along a narrow access road just to the east of the resort, and dropped Derek off a hundred yards or so down the rock cliff coastline.

"You sure you gonna' be okay?" Remmy asked as Derek climbed down from the van.

"Not really," the PI admitted. "But I'll give it my best shot."

"I've always got my cellphone on, if you need me."

"Appreciate it. Like I said, be ready to move fast if I do call."

From the drop-off point Derek made his way along the cliff, past a small grouping of pastel townhouse-style bungalows belonging to another resort (he waved at one surprised woman who'd been sunbathing topless by her private pool when he strolled past), until he crossed over onto Coral Queen property. He ignored the sign that warned trespassers of prosecution and found a spot amongst decorative grasses and palms where he could see the Geist bungalow clearly yet remain "persona non-see-um" – as he described his stealth stakeouts. He set-up a small portable listening dish and used a pair of video-recording binoculars to keep a close watch on the building.

He hated stakeouts. Even in the best of conditions, the boredom of watching a person, place, or thing for hours and sometimes days on-end was excruciating. Sitting in the midst of resort landscaping to keep watch – with biting insects as uninvited guests – was even worse. But Derek was determined.

Hours went by with no movement inside the bungalow. Derek used the downtime to review, and re-review his plan, even though he knew full-well he'd probably have to play it by ear before all was said and done. About three hours after he established the stakeout, he got a call on his cellphone.

"DiLaurain here," he answered.

"Mr. DiLaurain, it's Chief Inspector Trott. We got a hit on that motorcycle you wanted us to track down."

"And?"

"You were right."

"I knew it! It's all coming together now, Inspector."

"You're still a long way from being able to prove anything; you know that, right?"

"I do. But if all goes well, I should have enough soon to at least file charges."

"Then we'll keep our fingers crossed."

"You do that, Inspector."

Derek picked up his binoculars and scanned the small cottage. Nothing. He shifted his weight, trying to find a comfortable position on the rocky ground. No such luck.

Another two hours went by. As the sun arced slowly toward the turquoise water below, the insect life there in the shrubbery exploded in both intensity and volume. He swatted at some kind of flying pest that seemed to zero-in on his ears no matter how often he tried to shoo it away, but in seconds it was back. His lower back was beginning to ache, his shoulders were sore, and worst of all, he was getting hungry. He realized he should've brought more than just a few snack bars with him, but now it was too late. The growling of his stomach competed with the high-pitched whine of the insects congregating all around him.

Then, just as his patience was threatening to crack, the door to the bungalow opened and Mrs. Geist – dressed fashionably in a long black dress with pearl necklace and earrings – stepped out into the fading twilight. He slipped the headphones over his ears and turned up the volume gain.

"You sure you don't want to come?" the older woman asked someone in the bungalow.

"No, thanks Gran'ma. I'm not all that hungry," Alma's voice responded.

"You can't let that little squirt PI ruin your vacation!"

"It's not that…"

"Now don't start again! We've been over all that a dozen times – it had to be."

Derek glanced at the blinking green light, indicating he was recording.

"I know. It's just…"

"It's just nothing! You need to get on with your life. Things happen, but you can't let them determine who you are or who you're going to be. You know that."

The younger Geist stepped up into the doorway where Derek could see her. He lifted the binocs to his eyes and began recording video.

"I know Gran'ma..." The way she slurred her words made Derek think she'd either been drinking, or was taking some kind of tranquilizer, or both.

"Should I bring you back something?" Ida cut her off.

"Think they have ice cream?"

Mrs. Geist smiled. "That's better. I'll ask. Maybe get one of their people to run down to a local market if they don't."

"S' not really that important," Alma protested.

"Not a big thing. We'll see what we can do."

She leaned in and kissed her granddaughter on the forehead. "Now you try to rest. I'll be back as soon as your father and I are done eating."

"Don't rush on my account. I'll prob'ly take a nap." Now Derek was sure. She was zonked on something.

He waited patiently for Mrs. Geist to pick her way slowly along the cobblestone pathway, her cane picking out level spots for her unstable steps. At one point the old lady stopped and turned back to stare at the bungalow, her face a study in contemplation.

"Keep going, keep going," Derek muttered under his breath.

After a short period of reflection, she did.

The PI waited until she was well and truly gone before he fought his way out of the foliage and brushed himself off. He knew the next hour or so might well determine the course of his investigation, and he was ready. Double-checking that the two security thugs weren't lurking about, he made his way over to the bungalow door.

"Shave and a haircut, two bits," he sang to himself as he punched the buzzer with the kind of easy-going rhythm he hoped would lure Alma to the door. It did.

Her eyes opened wide the second she spied Derek.

"Mr. DiLaurain! I thought…"

"We should talk," Derek interrupted. "And I think you'd prefer it if your grandmother wasn't here."

"I don't…" she began, but the PI wasn't having any of it.

"I know about the motorcycle. You can either talk to me, or the police."

Her face froze. For just an instant Derek thought she might slam the door in his face. He could see conflicting emotions slide across her face. But then she let out a deep breath and opened the door.

"Okay. Let's talk."

The first thing he saw as he stepped into the suite was a couple of wine bottles on the breakfast nook table.

"Celebrating?" he asked, nodding toward the bottle.

She looked in the direction he'd indicated, confused.

"Wha'? Oh, no. Not celebrating." She sounded so down he almost felt sorry for her. "Def-nitely not celebrating."

"May I sit?"

"Oh, yeh, sure. Wherever you want," she said, sweeping her arm drunkenly across the entire room.

He waited for her to plop down on the sofa to his left before climbing up into the easy chair that faced her.

"Did you think we wouldn't trace the motor-cycle?" he asked before she could settle herself.

"I... I wore a wig. Our security guys gave me an ID."

"They had security cameras, Alma. We've got you on video renting the bike. What the hell were you trying to do anyway?"

She stared down into the empty wine glass she cradled in her hands. "We jus' wanted to scare you. Maybe get you to leave Bermuda." She didn't look up at him.

"'We'? Who else was involved?"

"No one! No one," she insisted, her shoulders hunched as if to ward off a blow.

He decided to let it slide. "Why? Why didn't you want me hanging around?"

She glanced up at him and then out the window. "You're a nosy little man. That's what Grandma says."

He'd planned to ease into the questioning, but in her current state he went for the jugular. "I know about the switch – in the wheelchair. I know it was your grandmother you wheeled back into your cabin onboard the Princess that night."

Her face went blank. "I... I don' know what you're talking about," she managed to sputter.

"I think you do. Why don't you tell me about it?"

She shook her head. "No. You're just guessin'"

Derek dug into the envelope he'd brought with him and pulled out the print from the ship's security video.

"It's not a guess. Here. That's your grandmother's bracelet."

Alma took the photo from his hands as if it were on fire and examined it closely.

"Doesn' prove anything," she muttered, whether to herself or Derek he wasn't sure.

"Oh, but I'm afraid it does. Your grandmother told me she'd designed it and had it made for her – a one of a kind piece. No jury would fail to understand what that means."

"Jury?" She looked as if she might be ill.

"Your father's death has been ruled a probable homicide. That means *someone* will be charged with his death."

"But..."

The PI had interviewed hundreds of witnesses and criminals. He'd developed a sixth sense about their breaking point. He knew Alma was faltering. It was time to close the case.

Just as he was about to put the pressure on, a key rattled in the front door.

All eyes swung in that direction.

"I brought you a... sweet," Mrs. Geist began before the door opened fully. "What the hell are you doing in here?!" she finished as soon as she saw Derek.

"Alma and I were just having a little talk. Isn't that right, Alma?"

When her grandmother turned toward her she was unable to speak.

"I've had quite enough of this, Mr. DiLaurain! I'm calling our security team. And then the police!"

"I don't think that would be a very good idea, Mrs. Geist." He took the photo from Alma's paralyzed hand and held it up for the old woman to see.

"*What* is that?" she asked, pausing with the phone in her hand.

"Look familiar? In particular, the bracelet."

Ida studied the photograph without commenting. She pulled herself stiffly upright, her head held high. Her expression never wavered.

"Doesn't mean a thing," she said after a long delay.

"That's what I said!" Alma offered, snapping out of her drunken frightened daze.

"Do you remember when we first met?" Derek asked the elder Geist. "You told me you designed the bracelet yourself. That means there's not another one like it in the world. Certainly not one that Mr. Geist would wear. I checked with Arnie. You husband wouldn't be caught dead wearing jewelry."

"The video isn't clear – it could've been any bracelet." She didn't sound quite as certain as just moments earlier.

"It's clear enough. And with some digital processing, it can be made even clearer." Derek had no idea if that was true, but he knew the average person had seen so many detective shows that they'd believe almost anything about digital wizardry.

"No one would believe you," Mrs. Geist said in little more than a whisper. She sounded downright shaky.

"No? Let's see if Chief Inspector Trott agrees with you." He took out his cellphone as if to call, but Mrs. Geist was having none of it.

"No!" she cried out, hobbling toward him faster than he would've thought possible.

"Why not? If there's nothing to it…"

Derek watched the old lady's eyes dart back and forth in a panic. Then, like a Thanksgiving Day balloon with a pinprick hole, she deflated into the little old lady she was.

"You don't understand," she sighed weakly.

"Then tell me, make me understand."

"Don' do it, Grandma!" Alma said, her voice terror-filled.

"It's either that, or I call the Inspector," the PI repeated.

"I need a drink," Ida said, turning to Alma. "Do you have any more of that wine?"

At first her granddaughter didn't understand, or didn't believe what she was hearing.

"Wine – do we have any more wine?" the old lady repeated.

"Ye'sh, sure," the granddaughter finally answered, walking numbly to the half-empty bottle and pouring a glass.

Derek and Ida watched in silence as Alma made her way back to them, her steps unsteady.

"You should sit down," her grandmother ordered. "You too," she added to Derek.

All three of them found seats, Ida collapsing into hers with an audible groan. She took a long sip of her wine before turning to Derek.

"Oh, I'm sorry, can we get you anything?" she asked when she realized he was empty-handed.

"No, thanks," he said. He sensed they were on the verge of a break, and didn't want to give any reason for back-pedaling.

Ida nodded and took a deep breath. "This is all off-the-record, understood? You tell anyone what was said here, and we'll both call you a liar."

Derek nodded. He wasn't about to promise her any such thing, but he wasn't going to contradict her either.

"So you think you know what happened that night on the Princess, is that right?" she asked.

"I have a pretty good idea. But why don't you tell me what really went down."

She glanced over at Alma, who looked like a frightened little bird. She turned back toward the PI and continued.

"Let's say, hypothetically you understand, that once upon a time there was a very wealthy and powerful man. A giant in his business life. But this man, he had problems in his personal life. Real problems. His family knew he was a little *off.* I mean, too much into business and too little involved with people. His wife and children in particular. Almost as if the family was... an irritant that had to be tolerated. You understand?"

Derek nodded.

"Yes, well this man, this hypothetical man, he..." she fidgeted with her bracelet, turning it back and forth on her wrist as if adjusting a handcuff, "he became more and more distant over the years, so that by the time his first granddaughter was born, he rarely spent any time at home other than to sleep and perhaps eat an occasional meal."

She looked to Derek, who kept his eyes on hers but showed no emotion whatsoever.

"Although he acknowledged the granddaughter in his will and kept a picture of her on his desk at work, he didn't show her any more... interest than any other member of his family – not his children, not his wife." She took another long drink of her wine and looked down at the floor. "Until the granddaughter's eleventh birthday."

"Grandma, no!" Alma suddenly cried out. Her eyes were already red and tearing.

"Why don't you go lie down," Mrs. Geist said softly. It was more an order than request.

Alma looked lost, confused, but pushed herself up from her chair and staggered off as directed. Ida waited until the door to the bedroom closed with a loud thud.

"Do you have any grandchildren, Mr. DiLaurain?" she asked out of the blue.

"Don't have any kids," Derek said.

"Yes, well children are wonderful. They give your life a dimension you can't even fathom until you actually have one. But they also bring worry, and fear, and occasionally even heartbreak. It's a mixed bag." She looked into the far distance as if she could see images from her past out there somewhere. "Now grandchildren," she went on, looking back toward the PI with a tiny smile, "grandchildren are another thing altogether. All the things you did wrong, all the hopes and aspirations you had for your own kids that didn't come to pass – you try to correct all that with your grandchildren. Best of all you can give them back to their parents when they misbehave." The smile got a bit broader. "It's a wonder." She shook her head gently, the smile genuine and lingering.

But then it was gone. "You don't… you can't imagine anything bad happening to them – do you understand?"

Derek nodded. He realized he'd been holding his breath.

The old woman took another sip of wine, and hesitated. She looked as though she wanted to say more, but when she tried to speak her lower lip trembled ever so slightly.

"They say grandkids are the one silver lining to old age," he said, trying to give her time to collect her emotions.

"Yes, yes that's true," she said, swallowing and then licking her lips. "So, when a man, a man you think you've known for many, many years, when a man does something bad to a grandchild, you might not even notice it. You might think the grandchild was going through a phase, or whatever. But that's not always the case." The old lady's face suddenly became hard, fixed, a scowl on her lips.

"There are men, from all walks of life, men who..."she stopped, trying to find the right word, "...*crave* young girls. Did you know that, Mr. DiLaurain?"

Her naiveté surprised him; the pain in her voice made him wince. He nodded solemnly.

"I didn't know. Or, at least I didn't think about it. I don't know..." She stopped again, looked down at her hands for several long seconds, and then took another sip of wine.

"These *men*," she spit the word as if it burned her tongue, "they have clubs. That's what they call them –

clubs. They trade pictures, videos…." Her voice drifted off. She took a deep breath. "And girls. They trade *girls*." She looked up at him with tears drifting down her cheeks. Her eyes fell once again to her hands; she sat silent for an uncomfortably long period.

"This man, the business man. Was he that kind of person?" he asked quietly when he began to fear she might not go on.

Her shoulders shook as if the effort to answer was almost too much to bear. "Yes." She began to sob silently, her head dropping limply to her chest. The near-empty wine glass fell from her hands, spilling the last few drops on the rug – the red spattered pattern a sight he'd seen many times in very different circumstances. He waited for her to compose herself, but when she didn't he climbed down from his seat and went to her side. He put his arm round her shoulder, hugging her gently to his body. She turned her face and buried it into his chest, her sobs becoming more and more vocal.

Derek heard the door open and footsteps come running before he saw Alma.

"What're you doin'?!" she screamed in a panic. "Leave her alone!"

She hurried as best she could to where her grandmother sat sobbing, pushing Derek aside and cradling the elderly woman in her arms.

"Shh, shh, it'll be okay," the young woman cooed as if to a small child. "It'll all be okay."

Derek waited patiently, acid rising in his throat. After a minute or two, Ida regained control and sat up, wiping her eyes.

"I'm sorry. I just…"

"You don' have to 'pologize to *him*," Alma spat with drunken vehemence.

"It's alright," the older woman said, stroking her granddaughter's hair. "I was just telling Mr. DiLaurain about a hypothetical businessman I once knew."

Alma looked at her grandmother with obvious confusion.

"I don' understan'," she slurred.

Ida patted the young woman on her arm. "Why don't you go back to your room, honey? I need to talk to Mr. DiLaurain alone."

Alma glanced at Derek and then back at her grandmother. "I can stay if you wan'."

Ida forced a smile. "No, I don't think that will be necessary. Why don't you go lie down for a while longer? I'll come get you when we're done here."

Her granddaughter nodded woodenly. "Okay."

Ida helped her to her feet and half-led, half-supported her back to her bedroom.

By the time she returned, the old woman had regained her self-control completely.

"Sure I can't get you anything to drink?" she asked the PI.

"You don't have a beer by any chance, do you?" he asked. He could use a drink right about then.

Ida went to the wet bar and took a beer from the mini-frig. "Bud okay?"

"Great. Thanks." Funny enough, Derek felt intimidated by the old woman. Something about the way she carried herself with so much control so soon after her little breakdown.

Mrs. Geist handed him the bottle and a glass, then sat in a high-backed chair directly across from his.

"We were talking about that businessman, I believe," she said, her voice impossibly calm and modulated.

He took a long sip of the beer. "We were. About his predilection for young women."

"*Girls*," she corrected. Her eyes were cold, hard. "His predilection for girls." She leaned back into the chair. He waited. She closed her eyes and began again, softly, trancelike. "People like this businessman, they hide their real feelings, their sickness. They make you think that they're like other people, that they love their grandchildren like normal people. But they don't. They *use* them. And they let their friends *use* them. They are like animals." She stopped for a second and Derek thought she might begin to cry again. But she did not.

She swallowed and took a deep breath. "Perhaps
their family should recognize the signs, should see
through their mask at the monster behind it. But…" she
stumbled, "…sometimes they don't. They don't see
what's happening right in front of their eyes. And the
poor little ones are too afraid, too confused to say a
thing." She stopped again, took one deep breath, sat up
straight and went on. "This sort of thing can go on for
years. *Many* years. Until finally, maybe a long time after
the… abuse takes place, something happens and the
family finds out about the businessman. Maybe they
learn that he's taken a very large sum of money from the
company coffers, and find out that the little granddaughter wasn't the only one – the only one he'd
molested. There were others. And the businessman
wants to pay them for their silence, to *buy* their
innocence." The words came faster now, in a flood of
pent-up emotion, guilt, and pain. "He thinks he can buy
his freedom, buy his reputation in the community. And
the family is faced with a terrible dilemma – do they
destroy everything the businessman has created in his
lifetime? Do they endanger the future of the very
grandchild he abused? It wouldn't un-do what had been
done. It wouldn't make the others whole again, but it
would make them rich. Perhaps allow them to move
past it…" She seemed to be arguing the point with
herself as much as with Derek. "So they don't say

anything. They don't show they know what horrors this... businessman has inflicted." She looked up at him with a stare that chilled his blood.

"But they cannot let it go unpunished."

She looked away but said no more.

The PI waited a short while before nudging her gently. "Did *all* the family know about the businessman's... activities?"

For a long moment he thought she might not respond. But then she looked back into his eyes, her stare unforgiving. "Not all. Just the granddaughter and his wife. Just the two of them."

It was all becoming clear now. He could imagine the two of them plotting to *punish* the businessman. Booking the cruise, timing the route, assigning roles.

He had to ask.

"Did they? Did they punish the businessman?"

Her eyes danced back and forth. "Just the wife," she whispered. "The girl didn't know. She wasn't told."

Now her eyes pleaded to be believed.

He knew she was lying, or at least his every instinct told him she was. But he understood.

"A sad story," he said.

"What are you going to do now, now that you've heard my story?"

Derek couldn't hold her stare and looked away. "I don't know. I'll need to think on it."

The old woman nodded. "I see. Just remember, the young girl has already been punished – many times. She shouldn't have to deal with all that pain, not again."

Derek didn't know what to say. Without a formal admission of guilt it was far from certain she could be convicted. She was old. She could afford the best lawyers. The evidence was all circumstantial. If she denied that Alma had participated in the crime, the granddaughter would almost certainly go free. The man had been a monster. He probably deserved to die. But did they have the right to act as judge, jury and executioner?

"I'm sorry to have put you in this position," Ida said, jarring him from his train of thought. "I realize you're in a difficult situation." She might have been trying to butter him up, but he believed her.

"Yeh, well I guess we all are, in different ways."

"Are you going to go to the police?"

"I don't know," he said honestly. He didn't know what he would do.

She pinched her lips together as if struggling to restrain herself. "All right. I suppose that's the most I could ask for. Will you let me know – when you've made your decision?"

"Yeh, sure. I think I can do that."

"Thank you." She struggled to her feet. "Now, I need to lie down."

He climbed down off the chair. "I'm not going to run into your two goons outside, am I?" he asked.

She looked at him as if she didn't understand the question. "Goons? Oh, the two security people. No, they'll be dismissed. Not much reason anymore."

"Good evening then," he said. He couldn't think of anything else to say.

"Good evening to you, Mr. DiLaurain." Her voice seemed tired, so very tired.

He let himself out. Without really planning to do so, he found himself wandering down to the cliffs overlooking the sea. He stood there for quite some time, staring out as line after line of rolling waves broke upon the pinkish sand below, a blood-red sun sinking beneath the horizon's razor edge. Then it grew dark, and a cool breeze swept in off the water; he finally shook his head clear and headed back to his room.

*****

Olga was upset.

"Where you have been?!" she asked as soon as he stepped into the suite.

"Had a little talk with Mrs. Geist."

"You *still* work on that case? I thought she fire you."

"You know I never give up on a case until it's solved."

She sighed. "I know. Did old lady say something that help?"

He shrugged. "I don't know if it helped or made everything a million times harder."

She muttered what he recognized as a Russian swear word. "Too much. Beside, I am hungry."

He glanced at his watch. It was nearly eight. No wonder she was hungry.

"Give me twenty minutes," he offered.

"I give you punch in nose," she said, and he felt she was only half-joking.

*****

"That's one hell of a screwed-up situation," Brady said when he heard Derek's description of his meeting with Mrs. Geist. "What're you going to do?"

"I don't know. Part of me wants to turn her in to Inspector Trott, but the other part sees no value in it. She's no threat to society, and never will be. It's got me tied-up in knots. What would you do?"

A long pause. "Geist was a monster. No question. But people shouldn't push other people off the side of ships, monsters or not."

"That's the dilemma. What's your answer?"

"You never make it easy, do you?"

"You'd get bored if I did."

The PI could almost feel his friend pondering over the phone line. "Let sleeping dogs lie," he finally said. "No good will come of telling your Inspector, only heartache."

Derek nodded to himself. He realized he'd been hoping for just that response.

"Only thing is, I've sort of got Trott all revved up to solve the case," he said "How do I get him un-revved?"

This time Brady's response was much faster. "Tell him the truth, sort of." And then he explained.

*****

"Inspector, I hope it's not too late," Derek said when Chief Inspector Trott answered his cellphone just a few minutes later.

"No, no problem," the Bermudian said with little conviction. "What's up? Did you get a break in the case?"

"Not exactly. As a matter of fact, pretty much the opposite. You know that green bracelet I told you about? Turns out Mrs. Geist designed one for her husband. A little less feminine, but the same basic look." He'd have to get to Mrs. Geist and *remind* her of her gift before the Bermudian cops talked to her again.

"So it could've been him in the wheelchair all along."

"I'm afraid so."

"Damn! I was hoping that little bauble would lead us to something solid. I'm getting a little tired of chasing my tail on this one."

"Yeh, looks like we're back to square one," Derek said, feigning resignation.

"Not quite square one. We've got the DNA team heading out to swab the family members tomorrow. Maybe we'll get something from that."

"Maybe. I guess we'll know soon enough."

They chatted for another few minutes, but it was clear the Inspector had had enough of the Geist family for one day. And since Derek had no more red herrings to plant, the conversation ended rapidly.

As soon as Trott hung up, Derek dialed Mrs. Geist's bungalow. To his surprise, she answered.

"Mrs. Geist – don't hang up! It's me, Derek."

"I know who you are," she said, sounding even more exhausted than when he'd been there.

"I just got off the phone with Chief Inspector Trott."

"Couldn't wait to tell him, is that it?" If misery were a sound, it was her voice at that moment.

"Actually, I told him that you designed a green bracelet for your husband much like the one you often wear."

"Why?" she managed to mutter.

"I'm not sure. But it might make his investigation a little more complicated."

A long pause. "Will it help us?" The hopefulness in her voice stung him.

"I don't know. It might. But he's sending a team out to your resort tomorrow to take DNA swabs from you and Alma – the whole family. I thought you'd want to know."

"DNA? Why?"

"As I think I mentioned, your husband had some skin and blood under his fingernails when they found him. They hope to match the DNA with someone from the family."

He heard a short gasp. "If they make the match?"

"It would be bad." He didn't want to get into it too deeply. An angry prosecutor could already try to nail him for tampering. He wasn't going to stick his neck out too much further.

"I see." She was quiet for so long, Derek thought she might have hung up. But she hadn't. "Thank you, Mr. DiLaurain," she said at last. "Maybe I was right in hiring you after all."

"I... I hope it works out for you, and your granddaughter," he said. "Goodnight, Mrs. Geist."

"Goodbye, Mr. DiLaurain." The phone went dead immediately.

He slowly disconnected on his end, his mind struggling to see a way clear for the old lady and her granddaughter. After a long moment of thought he slipped the phone into his pocket and made his way to the adjoining room, where an impatient – and hungry – Olga waited.

"Everything good?" she asked when she saw him come in, his face twisted with concern.

"I don't know," he admitted. "But it's as good as it can be for now."

*****

The restaurant was decorated with dark wood, old, classic silver and dozens of flickering candles. A pianist played soft, romantic music as a dozen or so well-heeled diners chatted and nibbled and drank expensive wine. The food smelled good, and Olga certainly demonstrated the hunger she had so diligently complained about. Derek tried to keep a contented look on his face, despite the direction his thoughts had taken.

He knew he should eat, but his appetite had vanished.

CHAPTER 15

Derek awoke to the sound of screaming sirens moving west in the early morning light. There was no reason for him to think twice about the plaintive wail, but he did. Something made him sit up in bed, shake the cobwebs from his head, and dial the Geist bungalow at the Coral Queen. The phone rang, and rang, and rang. He felt the tingling sensation that always accompanied an intuitive flash. He got up and threw on his clothes, not even bothering to awaken Olga.

It was too early to call Remmy, so he jumped in a cab he found sitting outside the reception area.

"Coral Queen," he said.

"You got it, Boss," the cabbie answered with a stifled yawn.

In the gray pre-dawn light the roads to the resort were nearly empty, just a scooter here and there and the occasional late-nighter or early-riser. It took less than fifteen minutes to reach the resort. The driveway was partially blocked with police cars and an ambulance, their red and blue lights flashing relentlessly, reflecting off the palms that lined the entranceway.

"Can you wait?" he asked the driver.

"If you can pay, I can wait."

Derek scrambled down from his seat, hurried past two local cops questioning the desk clerk, headed straight for the Geist bungalow. Long before he saw the low-slung building he knew in his gut that all the activity was centered on their little cottage. The only questions were who and what?

A Bermudian policeman stopped him before he could get within twenty feet of the building.

"Sorry sir – police matter."

He pulled out his PI ID. "I work for Mrs. Geist," he said officiously. "I'm supposed to meet with her this morning." He was stretching the truth, but it was the quickest way to get where he needed to go.

The cop inspected his ID closely. "A little early for a meeting, isn't it?"

He changed tack. "Is Chief Inspector Trott here, by any chance? He can vouch for me."

The officer eyed him with a dubious frown. "The Inspector is inside. Wait here."

He took Derek's ID and went into the bungalow. Derek saw an anthill of activity inside during the few seconds the door remained open. Trott came out moments later.

"Mr. DiLaurain. You had an appointment with Mrs. Geist?"

The PI ignored him. "What's going on, Inspector?"

Trott hesitated as if debating whether to answer. "It's Mrs. Geist. She's dead."

Derek's stomach fell. "Dead?! How?"

"Not sure yet. But it looks like suicide. You don't have any idea why she might kill herself, do you?"

"No, no I don't," he lied. Unless the authorities forced him to reveal his conversation with the woman, he intended to keep it to himself.

"I gotta tell you, I don't like this. Not one bit. First her husband, now her. I..." He was about to continue, when Arnold Jr. came out of the bungalow carrying a white envelope.

"Inspector. Mr. DiLaurain!" he added when he spied the diminutive PI. "We found this slipped under our door," he said, handing the envelope to Trott.

"Have you read it?"

"Haven't even opened it. Thought you'd want to see it first."

"Do you recognize the handwriting?

Arnie took a deep breath. "Appears to be my mother's."

"Thank you. If you'll excuse me for a minute…" He went back into the bungalow, leaving Derek and Arnie on the walkway outside.

"I'm sorry for your loss," the PI said as soon as they were alone.

Arnie nodded solemnly. "Thank you. It's so… unexpected." They stood there in contemplative silence for a second, until the eldest Geist son recovered and reached into his back pocket to pull out another envelope. He handed it to Derek. It was addressed to him in a neat cursive script. "She apparently left this for you."

He glanced at it briefly. "Any other notes?"

A flicker of anger, or perhaps disappointment, passed over his face. "No. Just the two." When Derek didn't comment, he went on. "Do you know why she would leave you a note?"

"I'm… not certain," he said. This was no time to get talkative. "But, maybe we should keep it to ourselves. Agreed?"

It was clear that Arnie had his doubts, but he nodded. "As long as you let me know what it says."

"You might not want to know."

"So you do know something," he began, but just then Inspector Trott came back out of the suite.

"Mr. Geist, Mr. DiLaurain: it looks like we now know what happened to Mr. Geist."

"How do you mean?" Arnie interrupted.

"I'm sorry to have to tell you this, but that note you gave me *was* from your mother. She admits to having been present when your father went overboard…"

"What!? I don't believe it!"

The Inspector handed the letter to him. "I'm afraid it's true. Read for yourself." He turned to Derek. "She says he fell overboard trying to hit her when she confronted him about some 'past indiscretions' she didn't want to innumerate. Claims Alma only became involved after the fact. What do you think?"

"If that's what she said, I suppose that's what happened."

"I still can't believe it," Geist said as if in a daze.

"It *is* surprising," Trott agreed.

"What about the granddaughter?" Derek asked. "What are you going to do about her?"

The Inspector shook his head. "Question her, I suppose. Beyond that, I'll have to discuss it with the Prosecutor's office."

"From what Mrs. Geist said in the note, at the worst you could only get her as an accessory after the fact, and you probably couldn't prove she knew anything even then. Hard case for little return." He wondered if the recently-departed Mrs. Geist could somehow sense he was still working for her.

Trott looked at him closely. "Not my call."

"I'm sure the Prosecutor will take your advice into consideration."

"Do I take it you wouldn't favor charging her?"

"Not *my* call. But I don't see the purpose, the *public good*."

Trott nodded. "I suppose I agree. Perhaps I should go talk to her."

Arnie suddenly came back to life. "I'm sorry, Inspector. But any conversations with my daughter will have to be in the presence of her lawyer."

Trott grimaced. "Will you give me your word you'll make sure she stays on the island until we sort all this out?"

"Of course. We aren't going anywhere."

Derek bit his tongue. In DC there'd be no way a cop would take the word of a possible perp that they'd hang around town waiting for a warrant to be issued. But this wasn't DC.

"All right then. I'll go meet with the DPP and we'll figure out what we're going to do next. I'll be back in touch with you as soon as it's decided."

"Thanks, Inspector. As you can imagine, Alma has been shattered by her grandmother's death. I only hope she'll have some time to get over it." It was clear he was fishing for the Inspector's intent.

"I can't promise anything. We'll see."

With a mock salute the Inspector left – Mrs. Geist's note in hand – having stationed police at both entrances to the bungalow and at the head of the path that led to it.

"What a mess," Arnie said as he watched Trott walk away. "I'm numb. Can't even believe it."

"Believe it," Derek said softly.

Arnie turned toward him with a startled look. "You knew?"

"Some of it. Enough."

"But why? What could possibly make her do such a thing?"

"I... I'm not sure," he said. If the old lady wanted to keep the reasons secret, who was he to reveal the family's dirty laundry?

"What does the letter say – the one she addressed to you?"

"I'll let you know when I've read it. For now, I think it might be a good idea if I speak with Alma."

"She's resting. My mother's death hit her hard."

"Even so. Inspector Trott might be back here in short order. We should talk."

"I'll go with you..."

"I don't think that's a good idea." To his questioning look, Derek added, "They can't question you about something you didn't hear."

Arnie grudgingly agreed to let the PI talk to his daughter. Derek went into the bungalow, found a quiet corner and skimmed the note from Mrs. Geist. It said pretty much what he expected it to say. He knocked gently on Alma's door and found her lying in bed, her shades drawn.

"Alma, are you awake?" he asked softly.

"I don't want to talk to you, Mr. DiLaurain," she answered, her voice low, in pain.

"I'm sorry, but I'm afraid we have to talk. Your father okay'd it."

She sat up in bed. "My grandmother is dead. She *killed* herself. Can't you just leave me alone?"

"I wish I could, but it's only a matter of time before Inspector Trott is back here with more questions – some very tough questions, unless I'm mistaken."

"What do you mean?" She sounded like a little girl, lost and afraid.

"Your grandmother left me a note," he said, pulling the envelope from his pocket for emphasis. "She explained everything."

Alma's face, which had been drawn, fell into a blank stare. She swallowed. "Everything?"

"Look, I'm not here to judge you. I understand you and your grandmother had... *reasons* for what you did. But I'm not certain Inspector Trott – or the

Prosecutor – will feel the same way. So we need to talk, about that night."

"Okay." She stared wide-eyed. He climbed up on the end of her bed facing her.

"Your grandmother said she knew you took your grandfather for a walk every night before bed, and she planned to have it out with him on that particular night, in a place where they wouldn't be overheard. She said it was because she found out about him embezzling $200 million from their company to pay off past *liaisons*. She wanted you close-by because she thought your presence might help keep his temper under control. He had a *very* bad temper. Are you following?" She looked so out of it, he was afraid she wouldn't remember the plotline Ida had invented. She nodded. "Okay, so she went up there hours before you two did, and waited for you to come up. When you got up there she watched you from a hiding place for a while as your grandfather sat by the railing looking out at the stars and sea, and then intercepted the two of you as you were on your way back to your cabin. She said she was getting worried, you'd been up there so long. It was so cold she sent you to get a shawl she'd draped over a deckchair a hundred feet or so down the deck. You went to get it but when you were almost there you heard a brief shout and came hurrying back. When you got there your grandfather was gone. She told you she'd confronted him about the theft from the company, and in a fury he'd tried to stand and hit her and had lost his balance and fallen overboard. You asked her to report it so they could stop the ship, but she convinced you that he was long gone and it would only cause problems for the family and the business. She collapsed into the chair and you pushed her back to the suite, having sworn to keep the secret. Then she wrote a confession and took a handful of sleeping pills.

"Do you understand?"

"But…" she began; he held up a hand to stop her.

"Your grandmother is dead. She is the only person who could say it happened differently than that. So that's how it happened. Right?"

For a long time the young woman stared at Derek, or more accurately past him at something, or nothing, only she could see.

"Yes, I understand," she finally mumbled.

"Tell me. Tell me how it happened." He listened patiently, reminding her of some details as she regurgitated the story of her grandfather's death. "Good, that's very good," he said when she finished the telling.

She said nothing for several seconds. "You *know*," she said, shaking off the lethargy, "don't you?"

"I wasn't there. All I know is what your grandmother told me in this note. Oh, and one more thing." He pointed to some nasty scratch marks on her upper arm. "If anyone asks, you got those earlier that night when you were helping your grandfather get into his wheelchair back in the room and he lost his balance. He said it was probably from the sleeping pills he'd taken."

She stared at her arm and her cheeks turned a bright red. When she finally looked at him again she had regained a good deal of her composure.

"Why?" she asked.

"How do you mean?"

"Why are you doing this? You know what happened."

Derek cocked his head off to one side. "Like I said, I only *know* what Ida told me."

"You have your suspicions."

"I was hired by your grandmother to find out what happened to her husband. He fell overboard. Case closed."

Alma pondered his words. "She did this – she killed herself – for me, didn't she?" Her voice wavered as tears streamed from her eyes.

"For you, for herself, and for all the others. I think she couldn't let him live with what he'd done, but she couldn't live herself with what... she did. She was a good woman."

Sobs wracked her shoulders until Derek crawled over to where she lay and put an arm around her. It would be nearly an hour before she fell into a fitful sleep and he slipped silently from the room.

*****

Arnie had been waiting for him in the suite's living room, strangely quiet now that all the police and EMT personnel had left.

"She's asleep," Derek said to his worried look.

"You were in there for quite a while. What were you two talking about?" He tried to sound relaxed, but tension leaked through.

"We discussed the night your father disappeared. That note your mother left me pretty much spelled it out."

"And what did it say?"

Derek hesitated, debating exactly how honest to be with the guy. He decided to skirt the specifics unless pressed. "Basically she said she'd found out about some... other women he'd been with. A number of them over many years. When she confronted him he tried to hit her and fell overboard."

Arnie shook his head with a disgusted look. "Can't say it's a huge surprise. We all knew he must've been spending time with someone in the few hours he wasn't at the office. It sure wasn't us."

"She also said she believes the missing $200 million might have gone to them."

The disgusted look turned to fury. "What?! That SOB! That money wasn't his to take!"

"Apparently he thought it was."

Derek watched in silence as Geist paced back and forth.

When he finally stopped, his anger had tempered. "Mom killed herself over that bastard?"

"That's what she said. She blamed herself for his death, bastard or no."

He thought for a second. "Can I see the letter?"

"I'm afraid I destroyed it, according to her directions."

Arnie narrowed his eyes and looked about to say something, but apparently thought better of it. "So, what now?"

"For me, or you?"

"Both, I guess. I'm just so… discombobulated."

"It's understandable. I'd suggest you talk to your brothers, decide on the funeral arrangements – you'll probably have to coordinate with the U.S. Consulate here as far as getting her back to the States. And then, maybe get some help for Alma."

"How do you mean?" His concern was genuine.

"It's been a tough time for her. Losing both her grandparents, in such... unusual circumstances."

"Right. Of course. Maybe some of the other kids might need counseling as well."

"Probably a good idea to at least talk it over with them. See how they're handling it. Speaking of which, where are your brothers?"

"Aaron took off last night, back to the States. Didn't even let us know until he was on his way. Ayden is out and about somewhere here on the island. He must've gone out before sunrise."

"You'll break the news to him?"

Arnie nodded. "You know something, Mr. DiLaurain, my mother was right when she hired you. There's more to you than meets the eye." He realized his double entendre and colored. "I didn't mean..."

"No offense taken," Derek said with a smile. "I appreciate the thought."

"Once I get back to the office and all this sorts itself out, I think you'll be getting more than just kind words."

"Even better," the PI said, anticipating a bonus check in the mail.

"You're staying here, right?"

"I was. Your mother decided I was being a little too diligent in my efforts and sent me packing."

From his reaction it was clear Ida hadn't shared her concerns with him. "What? When?"

"A couple of days ago. We landed at a little place on the western end of the island. It's fine – no problem."

"If you'd like to move back here – we can arrange everything…"

"Nah. We're comfortable, and my girlfriend likes the view. But thanks anyway."

"Send me the hotel bill. As part of your expense account."

"Thanks. That's not necessary."

"I want to."

Derek shrugged. "All right. I'll have my assistant send it to you once we get back." He *was* his assistant, but no need to share that with Geist.

"Good. I don't know when we'll talk again…"

"Hard to say. But whatever the case, my condolences – for both your parents. Take care of yourself, and your family."

They shook and Derek headed off. He had one more very important stop before he could start his real vacation.

*****

Inspector Trott was not at all surprised to see the PI show up at his door.

"Mr. DiLaurain. I was wondering how long it'd be before we chatted again. Hadn't thought it'd be quite this soon."

"I wish I could say it's because I missed you..."

"No? So if it's not that, why do I have the pleasure of your company so soon after our chat at the Coral Queen?"

"May I sit down?"

"Uh oh. So this is going to take a while?"

"Depends."

"On?"

Derek scooted up into a chair. "Arnold Jr., the oldest of the Geist kids, gave me a note his mother had written."

"He didn't mention it to me," Trott groused.

"Well, it was addressed 'For My Eyes Only.' He was just following her request."

"And? What does it say?"

"Said. She asked me to destroy the note after I read it."

"And you did?" The Inspector was clearly not happy.

"She was my employer, and I didn't see that she wrote anything that could be considered material to her death – or her husband's."

"And you felt competent to make that decision?" Now he was getting snippy.

"Inspector, I've probably been involved in 500 investigations, half of which involved some kind of criminal offense. I think I know what's relevant and what's not."

Trott leaned back in his chair, lips pressed tight. "Okay. Nothing to do about it now. What did she say?"

"Basically reiterated what she'd said in the note you saw. Apologized for jerking me around. Said she'd arranged a bonus that'd be paid beyond what we'd agreed upon."

"That's all? Nothing specific about her husband's... accident?"

It was the first time Trott had referred to Arnold Sr.'s death as an accident, and for just an instant Derek was taken aback.

"Only that it'd happened when she'd confronted him about his indiscretions, and that she was sorry she'd dragged Alma into it."

"Dragged? Did she use that word?"

"I believe so. Yes, she did."

Derek could see the wheels turn in the inspector's mind. "Did she say when the girl found out what she'd done?"

"Not exactly. Just that she'd used the girl because she thought no one would suspect her if Alma was somehow involved."

"Used?"

"*Involved*, was probably what she actually said."

The Inspector's eyes narrowed as he watched Derek closely. If the PI had been just another Joe Schmuck, he'd've probably wilted right then and there. But Derek had been through dozens of such interrogations, and nothing the Bermudian could do or say was likely to catch him off-guard.

"Hmm. So not much to link the girl to her grandfather's murder, huh?"

"Not much at all. Looks to me like the old lady finally had had enough of her husband, used his nightly trip up on-deck to confront him, and then when things went south told Alma he'd fallen overboard. Probably made believe she was too shocked to walk and had the girl wheel her back downstairs. Maybe told her to keep quiet about the *accident* so the company's stock didn't suffer, or some such."

"Really? You think that's how it went down?" There was something about the Inspector's tone and expression that gave Derek a sudden case of dry-mouth.

"Might be. Don't know. Wasn't there."

"Funny, almost sounds like you were – there I mean. Except for an awful lot of maybes and probablies in your theory."

"Like I said, wasn't there." Derek knew enough to keep it short and sweet now that he'd made his point. Cops always wanted people to keep talking, figuring they'd put their foot in it sooner or later.

"Right." Trott looked up from the file he had on his desk and then closed it with something resembling finality. "So Geist cheats on his wife for what – 25 years? She finds out, decides there's no statute of limitations on being an asshole, and when she stands up to him onboard the cruise ship he takes a swing at her and gets dumped over-board. Then she gets the granddaughter to wheel her down to their cabin, looking a whole lot like old man Geist. And they don't say anything to anybody. Is that about it?"

"Best explanation I've heard."

Trott shook his head wearily. "Piece of crap, if you ask me. But the old lady's dead. She took the blame, and nobody's scrambling to extend the investigation further. If the Prosecutor agrees, we just might call this case closed."

Derek tried not to smile, instead nodding his understanding. "That might be best for all concerned."

"All? I don't know about that, but we don't have the resources to chase our tails for questionable returns.

I'll talk to Alma one of these days to confirm her grandmother's story, but barring some unexpected U-turn, I very much doubt there will be any charges levied."

"I'm sure the entire family will be relieved to hear that."

Trott looked out the window at the tourists and traffic moving past the headquarters building. "And you, Mr. DiLaurain – how do you feel about it?"

Derek shrugged. "Seems to me justice was served. And that's what we all want, isn't it: justice?"

Trott raised his eyes as if looking for divine inspiration, and then dropped them to stare intently at the PI. His voice was low, not entirely convinced.

"I suppose so, Mr. DiLaurain. I suppose so."

*****

"So now what?" Brady James asked when Derek had finished running-down the events of the past 24 hours.

"Not sure. For the immediate future, I intend to drink some cold beer, eat some seafood, and hang out at the pool or beach with Olga."

"In other words, your normal daily activities."

"Pretty much. Except here in Bermuda. I want to see if Trott follows-up with Alma, or if he just lets it go."

"What's your gut feeling?"

He hesitated. "Maybe 80-20 he does a pro forma interview and closes the case."

"So, everyone goes home happy, huh?"

"Except Mr. and Mrs. Geist. They go home in pine boxes."

"More like mahogany with gold trim."

"Still – don't think they're too happy about it."

"Touché. When can we expect your exalted presence back here in DC?"

"Uhh, maybe four or five days. Depends on how long it takes Olga to forgive me for ruining her vacation."

"Can you afford to stay out there that long? I thought you said everything costs an arm and a leg."

"Arnie's going to give us a little bonus. Should more than cover our stay."

"Including beer?"

"It'll be tight, but I think we can swing it."

"I have a feeling that's not the only thing that's going to be tight. Watch yourself. I don't want a phone call in the middle of the night begging to bail you out."

"Turn off your phone."

"I just might do that. I gotta run. Say hi to Olga."

"And to Anne."

"Will do. See you in a few days."

Derek hung up the phone and drifted out to the pool, where Olga lay face-down sunning in a bright yellow bikini that wouldn't have covered the little PI's biceps.

"You're getting good at this," he said.

"You come back," she said, not even bothering to lift her head.

"I did. And the Geist's are giving us a little bonus, so we can move back over to the Coral Queen, or anywhere else you'd like to go."

At that she finally looked up, shielding her eyes from the sun. "I like it here. Nice and quiet."

"Then we'll stay right here."

"For how long?" A hint of distrust colored her words.

"Four, five days. Whatever your little heart desires." He put his hand on her tanned backside and rubbed appreciatively.

"Can eat steak and lobsters?"

"All you want."

She lay back down without a word. Derek waited a few seconds, then stood as if to leave.

"Where you go?" she asked.

"I thought I'd throw on my swimsuit and come out here to join you."

She tilted her head just enough so one eye was visible. "Stay in room. Maybe I come join you. Then maybe come to pool and get sun - after."

He didn't have to ask 'after what'. One thing he loved about Olga: her appetites were all-inclusive.

The air-conditioning was blasting inside their suite, but he left the thermostat right where it was. As he slipped out of his clothes and into a hot shower, he couldn't help but think about poor Mrs. Geist and Alma. It seemed, to paraphrase one of his favorite songwriters, only the good get screwed.

He smiled. Maybe he was good after all.

EPILOGUE

It was their last day in Bermuda as a tanned and relaxed PI waited for his girlfriend to finish packing. He strolled out to the pool to take one last look at the turquoise waters in the distance. He'd miss the little island, despite all the bad juju that had gone-down during their stay.

"Penny for your thoughts," a familiar female voice said, startling him from his reverie.

He turned to find Alma Geist, wearing a white muslin blouse over a long casual blue skirt, standing beneath a beach umbrella off to one side of the pool.

"Alma! What a surprise."

"I was hoping to catch you out here alone. I've been by here a couple of times before but you were always... occupied."

"Oh? Something I can do for you?" He wondered if Trott was finally getting around to interviewing her.

"No. Not exactly. I just..." She stopped, whether unsure or afraid, he couldn't tell. "I just wanted to thank you, for everything."

"Just doing my job."

"I don't mean only that. Inspector Trott came out to the resort and asked me some questions. I told him what you told me to say."

"Good. Was he satisfied?"

"I think so. At least he said I could leave Bermuda whenever I wanted."

"If I were you, I'd make that sooner rather than later," he said. "Out of sight, out of mind. At least sometimes."

"We're leaving today. I'm going with my parents," she added.

Derek didn't say anything. He had a gut feeling she wanted to tell him something more. After a few seconds, she went on.

"He was an evil man," she said, her voice surprisingly strong. "Evil."

"Then I guess he got what was coming to him. Karma, you know?"

She looked down at the ground. When she spoke he could barely hear her, so quiet had she become. "Was it wrong? What we did?"

He took a deep breath. "I'm no one to judge you. Just a private investigator doing his job. But one thing I can say."

"Yes?" She looked up, the expectancy in her eyes touching a nerve.

"I've been in this business a long time. Good people are good people, even if they sometimes do things they might wish they hadn't. Don't beat yourself up. Just be the best person you can be and help someone else when they need it."

A small smile crept across her lips.

"Thank you." She walked over to him, bent down and kissed him on the cheek. "Grandmother said you were a smart man."

"You can fool some of the people some of the time," he said with a sly grin, a grin that he used to hide the feelings surging inside him.

"I don't know if we'll meet again…" she began.

"I hope so. But you never know."

"I hope so too."

With that she patted him lightly on the shoulder, turned and walked away to where a large black SUV waited for her. As he watched her go, Derek felt a sense of closure for the first time since old man Geist had disappeared.

"Hey, do we go or not?!" Olga called out from their room.

He turned to see her standing in the doorway, tall and elegant in what he assumed was a new pastel yellow sundress and a large sunhat shadowing half her tanned and immaculately powdered, glossed and blushed face.

"We go!" he said, and with one last look at the Atlantic in the distance, he went to collect his girl and be on their way.

Life was good.